Falling in Love Again

Jake led Nadia over to the couch. She snuggled up close to him and lifted her lips to his.

"Jake," Nadia gasped a few minutes later, pushing him away.

Jake raised himself up slightly, the world out of focus, his heart pounding. "Is something wrong?" he asked.

She lowered her eyes. "I try to pretend it is not so, but I am falling in love with you, Jake Collins."

Jake sat back on his heels and pulled Nadia up into his arms. "Nadia," he whispered, running his hand through her rumpled hair. As revelation dawned on him, he said, "I told myself this could not be happening. It's too fast. I'm on the rebound from Nancy. But Nadia, I'm not. *This* is the truth, the real thing. I'm in love with you."

NANCY DREW ON CAMPUS™

Available from ARCHWAY Paperbacks

Nancy Drew on Campus™ #23

Otherwise Engaged

Carolyn Keene

AN ARCHWAY PAPERBACK
Published by POCKET BOOKS
New York London Toronto Sydney Tokyo Singapore

AN ARCHWAY PAPERBACK *Original*

An Archway Paperback published by
POCKET BOOKS, a division of Simon & Schuster Inc.
1230 Avenue of the Americas, New York, NY 10020

Copyright © 1997 by Simon & Schuster Inc.
Produced by Mega-Books, Inc.

ISBN: 0-671-00215-5

First Archway Paperback printing September 1997

10 9 8 7 6 5 4 3 2 1

Cover photos by Pat Hill Studio

Printed in the U.S.A.

IL 8+

CHAPTER 1

Nancy Drew took the stairs two at a time. Please, Gail, be in, she fervently wished, but the *Wilder Times* office was dark. "Where are you, Gail?" she cried out in frustration. Her words seemed to echo through the hallway.

"Right behind you," Gail Gardeski answered.

Nancy nearly jumped out of her skin.

"You're here early," Gail commented. "Are you trying to make me look bad? I thought getting here by eight o'clock for the nine o'clock staff meeting was above and beyond the call of duty—even for the editor-in-chief." In fact, Gail looked as if she'd had a hard time getting out of bed that morning, her hair unbrushed and her raincoat rumpled as if she'd slept in it.

"I have a great lead," Nancy began as she turned on the office lights and followed Gail to her office. "I didn't want to wait for the meeting."

"Is it a nice, juicy scandal?" Gail asked, shedding her coat. "That's what we really need around here."

Nancy did a double take. Under her rumpled coat, Gail wore a soft blue tunic belted over leggings and a silk scarf of multicolored swirls. Suddenly her hair looked fashionably wild instead of unbrushed. Nancy felt a twinge of self-consciousness as she stood there in her jeans, flannel shirt, and old leather jacket. She shook back her thick red-blond hair and plunged ahead. "I sat in on a few chat rooms over the weekend. All anyone wanted to talk about was how to get in touch with the teaching assistants who had run an ad on the UseNet offering grades for cash at Wilder. Gail, this could be really big."

Nancy waited for Gail's enthusiastic reaction. It didn't come.

"That again!" Gail exclaimed. "Every semester the rumor mill coughs up the same old scheme. Whether it's an ad posted at the Student Union or on-line, there's nothing to it."

"But I talked to some students who corroborated the story. There was an ad on the UseNet from some TAs." Nancy couldn't believe that Gail would dismiss her idea out of hand.

"Nancy," Gail said impatiently. "You're not the first reporter on this paper to come up with this, and you probably won't be the last. Don't worry, I've got some decent assignments to hand out this morning. They'll keep you busy."

Nancy did not want another assignment handed to her. She wanted to follow her gut instincts and work on this story. "Gail, just give me some time to look into it, to find the ad on the UseNet at least. Give me a week, and if I come up empty, at least I'll have followed it through."

"Nancy, how can I make this clear?" Gail spoke in her editor-in-chief voice. "It's a waste of your time and effort, and the paper can't afford that." She irritated everyone, especially Nancy, when she became patronizing.

Unfortunately, Gail didn't stop there. "Sorry you lost an extra hour of sleep," she continued. "But you're not catching any worms with that story."

Nancy looked at Gail incredulously, then threw up her hands and walked out of her office.

An hour later, after a stiff double espresso for breakfast at Java Joe's, Nancy was back at the newspaper. Gail had already started the weekly brainstorming session. Nancy didn't look at her as she took a seat next to Jake Collins, her ex-boyfriend and main competitor for stories at the paper. "Right, Terrance, go with that lead," Gail was saying. "Anyone else?" She gestured to one of the sports reporters. "Candace?"

Nancy listened for a moment as Candace proposed a human interest story about the upcoming protest over cheerleaders' costumes.

Fluff! Nancy thought to herself, tuning out the rest of Candace's proposal. Sometimes Nancy couldn't figure out where Gail was coming from, and it made her mad. Gail talked about wanting real news, but shied away from anything controversial. Gail had told Nancy time after time that she was one of the two best writers on the paper. Still, she shot down at least half of Nancy's ideas, and Nancy was getting sick of it.

"Sometimes Gail is such a pain," she murmured under her breath, loud enough for only Jake to hear. "I'm sure if she'd let me run with my story I'd turn something up on TAs selling grades. What do you think?" Jake didn't answer. His head was bent over his notebook; he was reading a greeting card tucked inside. Nancy couldn't decipher the handwriting from where she sat, but below the signature was a string of little hearts drawn with a red ballpoint pen.

"Jake?" Nancy whispered.

He raised his head, shaking the dark, wavy hair off his forehead. "What?"

"Didn't you hear a thing Gail just said?"

Jake flashed a quick embarrassed grin. "Sorry. I kind of zoned out." As he shoved the card back into its pink envelope, a small photo fell to the floor faceup. It was a picture of Nancy's new suitemate, Nadia Karloff, a Russian exchange student who had moved in with Casey Fontaine after Stephanie Keats had moved out.

As Nancy bent to pick it up, she noted that even in a cheap arcade snapshot, Nadia was drop-dead gorgeous.

"Doesn't she look great?" Jake asked. Jake interviewed Nadia for the paper and had been dating her ever since.

"She does," Nancy admitted quickly, not wanting to seem to disapprove of Jake's new girlfriend. She eyed Jake carefully. His cheeks were pink, his eyes sparkled. He looked so— so alive. The very picture of a guy head over heels in love—with a woman he'd known for only a week or so.

It struck Nancy as weird that he had gotten so deeply involved so fast. That wasn't like the Jake she knew. Nancy fiddled with the belt loops on her jeans. Maybe that was why his relationship with Nadia felt slightly wrong to Nancy. A hot story lead or a gut-wrenching news piece could reel in Jake the reporter fast.

But when it came to feelings, Jake's ran deep and slow. At least, that had been Nancy's experience with him.

She handed the picture back to him. Maybe she couldn't be objective about this. Maybe she was just uncomfortable about Jake's having a new girl, and such an attractive one. Nadia was more than beautiful—she was exotic, too. Her jet black hair framed high Slavic cheekbones, liquid brown eyes, and full, expressive lips. Nancy had been initially intrigued by her appearance and her life story.

That was before Nadia had started dating Jake. Nancy still didn't know the girl very well. And ever since Nancy had run into Jake coming out of Nadia's room early one morning, Nadia had kept her distance. Nancy could sympathize, but secretly wished Nadia would transfer to another suite. It had been awkward for everyone in Suite 301 since Nadia started dating Nancy's ex.

Nancy watched Jake slip Nadia's photo back into the envelope, which was also covered with little hearts.

It was a little gooey for Nancy's taste, and didn't fit her image of Jake. But, hey, if Jake didn't mind the hearts and flowers routine, Nancy was happy for him. Or at least she would try to be.

*   *   *

"I hate this!" Stephanie Baur muttered as she stopped outside the five-story apartment house on Walnut Lane. She tossed her cigarette onto the snow-covered sidewalk, grinding it out with the heel of her high leather boot. With one hand grasping the heavy plastic grocery bag and the other holding the key in the lock, Stephanie pushed open the door with her hip. She stared glumly at the steep flight of stairs just inside the entranceway.

"Get with it, Keats—I mean Baur," she told herself, wondering if she'd ever get used to her new name. Stephanie sighed loudly before beginning the long trudge up to the fifth floor, where she lived with her husband of a few weeks, Jonathan Baur.

When she was dating Jonathan, she never noticed how dark and dreary the stairway was. Maybe because back then everything about Jonathan had been so intense and romantic that she hadn't stopped to notice the peeling paint on the walls and the steep steps, or how cramped his apartment really was.

By the time Stephanie reached the top of the stairs she was winded, depressed, and wondering how she could be the same person as the Stephanie Keats who had grown up surrounded by luxury and with a live-in maid.

"Steph? That you?" Jonathan flung open a door at the end of the hall, his handsome face wreathed in smiles.

7

In two strides he was by her side. He grabbed the heavy bag with one hand, and with the other, drew Stephanie close. "Missed you!" He buried his face in her thick dark hair.

Jonathan's touch sent a thrill from the bottom of Stephanie's feet right to the top of her head. "Me, too," she murmured, gazing up at him. Inside the apartment, Jonathan deposited the groceries on the kitchen table.

Before Stephanie could even take off her coat, he wrapped his arms around her waist. Jonathan traced the outline of her lips with a finger and studied her eyes. "You okay? You look tired or something."

Stephanie curled her fingers through the longish hair at the nape of his neck. "Tired, as in zapped." She leaned back in his arms. "It's been a wild day. First school, then half the customers at Berrigan's were on the warpath, and then the grocery shopping." She sighed. "Jonathan, I can't face the thought of cooking dinner. Can we order in?"

Jonathan stepped back and took Stephanie's hand. "Stephanie, we've talked about this. Take-out really blows our budg—"

"Don't say that word! You agreed to say 'spending plan,'" Stephanie snapped. A second later she seemed to have lost her fire. "Oh, what difference does it make? I hate both of them."

She crossed the small kitchen in a couple of

steps and went through the archway into the even smaller living room. Overnight, *cozy* had somehow become *claustrophobic*. Stephanie was beginning to despise their apartment. *Today's Bride* sure didn't show newlyweds in dingy digs like this.

"Come on, Steph. Things aren't so bad," Jonathan said. His calm, reasonable tone drove Stephanie crazy. "If we stick to our budg— spending plan, we can save money for things that really matter, like a house of our own someday."

"Someday," Stephanie grumbled, tossing her coat on a chair and plopping down on the saggy couch. "I can't see how one take-out dinner is going to affect what we spend on a house one way or the other." She fingered a hole in the frayed brown corduroy slipcover. Whatever had possessed Jonathan to put something so ugly in his apartment in the first place? It took up half the living room.

Jonathan walked behind the couch and kneaded Stephanie's shoulders. "Tell you what," he said. "I'll cook dinner." Stephanie began to relax. She touched his hand, leaned back, and looked up at him.

"Sounds good to me," she said, wondering how she had ever found such a sweet, considerate guy. "But you cooked dinner last night."

"I don't mind. My dinners might not be up

9

to the chef's standards at Les Peches, but maybe I'll surprise you."

"Surprises are good," Stephanie said. She could sure use one or two right now, she thought as she headed for the bathroom. She turned on the water in the tub, dumped in the last handful of her imported Dead Sea bath salts, inhaled, and wondered what part of their budget would let her buy more.

If I still look like a blimp, I'll just die, Bess Marvin told herself as she hurried past the bank of mirrors lining one wall of Hewlitt Center's dance studio. Bess was on her way to the costume department for a fitting, and though she had been starving herself for more than a week now, she felt fatter than ever. Keeping her eyes averted from the mirrors, Bess reached the costume room of Wilder's theater.

A short, round-hipped girl greeted her. "Bess. I almost gave up on you. Everyone else from *Cat on a Hot Tin Roof* has been here and gone. Rehearsal's in full swing already."

"Sorry, Amanda," Bess apologized to the theater major who was working as wardrobe mistress for the current production. "None of my scenes are scheduled until later. If you want I can come back tomorrow," Bess suggested, wondering if somehow she could lose another inch or two by then.

"No way." Amanda jabbed some straight

pins into the pincushion on her wrist and sorted through the costumes on a rack. "I altered Maggie's slip for you. It should be a perfect fit this time around."

"Right," Bess murmured as she changed into the slip.

Bess prayed silently before opening her eyes. She stared at her reflection in the mirror and couldn't see that she was any thinner. Her face was still too round, her arms too chubby. Her wavy blond hair tumbled over her bare shoulders. Bess sucked in her breath and touched the curve-hugging slip—and began to grin. It actually looked looser. Could it be true? Was her tummy really that much flatter? Bess turned first to the right, then the left. "YESSSSS!" She pumped her fist in the air and turned to grin at Amanda. "It worked. My diet worked."

"What's your secret?" Amanda patted her own plump waist and shook her head. "I never seem to be able to get rid of these ten pounds."

Bess smiled shyly. "I guess I was really motivated. I mean, can you imagine parading around onstage wearing only a slip and looking *fat?*" Bess shuddered.

"Fat?" Amanda scoffed. "Bess Marvin, you weren't the least bit fat to begin with. You have a great figure."

Bess left the fitting feeling high. She couldn't

believe all her dieting had paid off so quickly. Maybe she could afford to celebrate with a treat. Visions of the gooey chocolate brownies sold at the Cave danced through her head. Her mouth actually began to water. She hadn't eaten all day long.

Surely, just this once, a brownie wouldn't hurt.

CHAPTER 2

Jake Collins bounded up the steps to Suite 301, Thayer Hall, two at a time. His black cowboy boots clicked against the linoleum as he headed down the hall, whistling an old love song. The door to the suite was open.

"Anyone home?" he asked, poking his head inside. No one answered. The lounge was empty even though the TV was tuned to the evening news. Jake unzipped his leather jacket and headed for one of the rooms off the lounge, his heart starting to beat a bit faster. Man, Jake thought, you haven't felt so great since—he looked back over his shoulder at the door across the hall—you started dating Nancy.

This time, he was sure, he had gotten the romance thing right.

Jake knocked firmly on Nadia's door. "Nadia?" he called out. He thought he had heard her talking inside.

"Jake?" Nadia answered with surprise. She opened the door. She had on a dark green silk bathrobe. Her raven black hair spilled over the soft fabric at her neckline. Jake was at a loss for words.

"Am I early?" he finally asked. He put his hand on top of hers and started in the door. Nadia gently pushed him back. One of her delicately plucked eyebrows arched up. "No, don't come in. I am not ready yet," she said in her thick Russian accent.

"You look pretty good from here."

"You want me to go to dinner like this?" She pretended to be shocked.

"Noooo. Not exactly," Jake said. "But dinner can wait. . . ."

"Give me two minutes, Jake. I promise I will not disappoint you." She touched two fingers to her lips, raised them to his, and closed the door firmly in his face.

Jake stood there, feeling a little heady. "I doubt you could," he said to the door. He started for the lounge, then turned around. "Nadia?" he said softly, thinking she had called his name. "Nadia?" he repeated, a little louder.

"One minute, Jake," she answered. She then lowered her voice and continued talking. Had

Casey come home early from her long weekend? But there was only one voice—Nadia's. Jake thought the words sounded peculiar. Then it dawned on him: Nadia was on the phone, speaking Russian.

Who was she talking to? She had told him she was in the States to learn about America, not to hang around a bunch of homesick Russian students strumming guitars and singing gloomy Russian folk songs. So it was unlikely to be anyone on campus. He checked his watch. It would be the middle of the night in Moscow where her family lived.

"Jake?" Nadia sounded a little breathless when she came out several minutes later.

Jake looked up. "Wow!" he blurted. He forgot all about the phone call. Nadia walked over to him and wrapped her arms around his neck. "Worth waiting for?" she asked, her full red mouth lifted in a playful smile.

Jake breathed in the delicate scent of her perfume and touched her thick silky hair.

"Worth waiting for," Jake replied huskily, sealing her lips with his. Whatever else he was thinking got lost in a deep, passionate kiss.

Nancy waited in her room, her eyes scanning a battered copy of Jane Austen's *Pride and Prejudice,* which she was rereading for lit. class. But her attention wasn't on the novel—it was focused right outside her door. She didn't *want* to eavesdrop, but it was hard not to overhear Nadia and Jake. Kara Verbeck came in just then and greeted Nadia and Jake as they went out. Nancy listened as the familiar click of Jake's cowboy boots grew faint.

Finally the coast was clear. Nancy tossed her book on the bed, slipped into a green hooded sweatshirt, and went out to the lounge to catch the last of the evening news. Why does the Nadia-Jake thing bother me so much? she wondered. Nancy was frowning as she walked into the common room.

"Hi, Nan!" Kara, Nancy's roommate, greeted her. A bag of popcorn was popping away in the suite's microwave. "Didn't realize you were in our room. . . ."

Nancy forced a smile. "Who am I kidding? I was hiding until I was sure they were gone."

Kara nodded with sympathy. "You're doing better than I would. I mean, I'd probably remove myself to Pi Phi house and hide out for the next zillion years."

Nancy laughed. "It's not as heavy as all that. Jake and I are done, I'm really happy for him. We seem to be doing pretty well as friends these days." Nancy took the steaming bag of popcorn out of the microwave and joined Kara on the floor. Leaning back against the base of the couch, Nancy tried to sort out her feelings. Mad? Nope. Hurt? Definitely not. Jealous? No, Nancy didn't think so. Then what?

Kara dug into the popcorn, but kept her eyes on her roommate. "Okay, I believe you, Nancy. Of course, the fact that Nadia's such a nice person makes it easier."

"Mmm," Nancy mumbled through a mouthful of popcorn. *Nice* wasn't exactly the word Nancy would use to describe Nadia. *Puzzling? Mysterious? Fascinating?* Nadia was *nice,* but the word just seemed too plain for Nadia. She had a bigger-than-life quality—which Nancy admired. If it weren't for Jake coming into the picture, Nancy and Nadia might have become good friends.

As confused as ever, Nancy decided to sound out Kara. "Yeah, that was my take on her from the first time I saw her: almost too good to be true. The kind of person I'd like to get to know."

"Casey says she's heaven after Stephanie," Kara said, wiping her hands on her purple overalls.

Nancy smiled. "Nadia certainly improves the atmosphere around here, but I do miss Stephanie more than I thought I would."

Thoughtfully, Nancy put a piece of popcorn into her mouth. "Kara, tell me the truth. What do you really think about Nadia and Jake—as a couple?"

Kara shrugged. "They seem pretty happy together."

"That's true," Nancy admitted slowly. "Jake's

feet are barely touching the ground these days. And Nadia glows. So . . ."

"You don't sound convinced."

"I am," Nancy said easily. "You'd have to be blind not to see the way they look at each other."

"But—"

"But what?" Nancy asked, then laughed. "Kara, I wish I knew what was bothering me—"

"Besides the fact that Jake is half living across the hall from you with Nadia?"

"Yes," Nancy said, chafing her arms. "It's something else."

"Maybe it's that Jake barely knows Nadia. And no one else knows her any better. Or maybe you're jealous," Kara suggested.

"No way," Nancy insisted. "I'm happy for both of them. And I'll get used to running into Jake here after a while."

Nancy meant every word she spoke. Or was she just fooling herself?

Now, *this* was to die for! Bess told herself as she nibbled the remains of a double dutch chocolate brownie. She sat at a corner table in the Cave, a café in the basement of Rand Hall, which housed the architecture school. Consequently, the Cave was a favorite hangout with the "archie" and artsy crowd. It hummed busily for a Monday night. Senior industrial design drawings on the walls, avant-garde rock music in the air, and candles flickering on each table set the mood. Bess was glad for the noise, the dim light, and the fact that she hadn't run into anyone she knew. She had wanted to indulge in her brownie in private. Somehow calories didn't seem to count when no one saw her eating.

"O, churl! 'eaten' all, and left no friendly 'bite' to help me after?" Brian Daglian exclaimed, clutching his hand to his heart as he staggered up to Bess's table.

Bess laughed, but quickly crushed up the paper plate holding the last of her brownie crumbs. *"Romeo and Juliet,* Act Five, scene three. Except it's about drops of poison, not bites of brownie crumbs!" Bess teased her theater major friend, hoping he wouldn't think she had been pigging out.

"Ah, but my performance was good enough for you to recognize the source." Brian pulled up a chair, straddled it, and grinned at Bess. Blond, good-looking Brian had been cast to play Brick Pollitt, *Cat on a Hot Tin Roof*'s leading man, husband to Bess's Maggie. More than that, he was one of Bess's best friends at Wilder. "You really pulled Maggie's monologue together today. I told you you could do it," Brian said.

"I've had a good teacher," Bess stated simply, meaning Brian.

19

"So, our future is all set!"

"What future?" Bess eyed her friend dubiously.

"Bogey and Bacall. Astaire and Rogers. Marvin and Daglian."

Bess laughed with relief. "We sound like some kind of circus act."

"That, too," Brian remarked. "That brownie of yours really is all gone," he said, pushing his chair back. "I'm starved. Want another?"

"No!" Bess practically shouted.

"Hey, only asking. How about a coffee?"

"I'm sort of stuffed," Bess lied as Brian headed up to the counter. Actually, eating the brownie had made her twice as desperate for another one.

"So, ready for dress rehearsals?" Brian asked as he sat down again, putting a plate containing two brownies and a couple of cookies on the table.

Bess's mouth began to water. She pushed the plate toward Brian. "Right. I hope I can get used to wearing only a slip onstage."

"Believe me, you look pretty terrific in that slip, Bess," Brian said. "If I were straight, I'd propose to you right on that stage . . ."

Bess frowned. "Oh, great!"

"Really . . . forget about whatever that numero uno creepetto Daphne said about you being too chubby or whatever. You know, Maggie's not exactly supposed to look like

Teen Style's model of the year. You're perfect for Maggie, a real woman."

"I wish we could just skip opening night. In fact, I'm not sure I like the idea of an audience at all."

Brian snorted. "Come off it, Bess. Admit it. Deep down you adore the smell of the greasepaint and the roar of the crowd."

"Maybe not. Jeanne Glasseburg may have made a big mistake casting me as Maggie. I'm just a freshman!"

Brian's forehead creased. "And I'm not? Come on, it has nothing to do with your age. You're just worried that you can't pull it off, when you already *are* pulling it off. Believe me, Jeanne knew exactly what she was doing casting you. That woman's a pro in the theater world. Her seminar is a really big deal. She wanted you in her classes, and she asked you specifically to audition for the role. She knew you'd be a perfect Maggie."

Suddenly Bess had an image of herself all chunky and lumpy in Maggie's slip. She tried to calculate the exact calorie count for one brownie. After a moment of mental arithmetic, Bess felt her stomach knot up.

"Hey, Marvin, are you listening or what?"

"Sorry." Bess smiled nervously at Brian. "I zoned out there."

"I was saying the press sometimes actually comes to Wilder openings."

"The press." Bess's heart stopped. "You're kidding, right? You mean someone from the *Wilder Times.*"

"And the Weston *Daily Herald,* usually one of the Chicago papers, and sometimes a stringer turns up from LA or New York."

"We'll be reviewed by *real* papers." Bess was appalled.

"We, my dear, are heading for the big time and—"

Bess had stood up abruptly.

"Hey, Bess, where are you going?"

"I've got to go. It's getting late, and I've got to go for a run."

"Run as in jog?" Brian gaped at Bess.

Bess managed to look smug. "Aren't I allowed?"

Brian regarded her skeptically. "When did you get into the fitness thing?"

"Uh . . . recently," Bess said. "Like just this minute."

Bess waved breezily toward Brian as she headed toward the door, her gastric juices on overdrive. He had joined friends at another table and had his back to her and the counter. Bess chewed the inside of her cheek, then hurried up to the counter. After all, except for that brownie she hadn't eaten a thing all day. "A calorie is just a calorie," she mumbled to herself.

"Three brownies to go, please." She quickly

handed the cashier her money, got her change and brownies, and stuffed them in the bottom of her knapsack, all the while praying that Brian wasn't watching.

"Let's party!" a voice boomed from the apartment next to Stephanie and Jonathan's. Music blared. Laughter came through the walls. The neighbors' doorbell rang again and again.

"I'm game," Stephanie muttered back at the wall. If only one of the grad students who lived next door would come over and ask, she'd be dressed in a moment, ready to dance the night away.

Instead, Stephanie sat in an overstuffed easy chair with her bare feet tucked up under her, trying to read her Psych 101 assignment. She had been at her homework since right after dinner and was more than ready for a break. In fact, she was ready for more than just a break. She was ready to cut out of here, to do something fun. Stephanie stole a glance at the sofa.

She growled softly under her breath. "Asleep?" She looked at the kitchen clock. It was just ten P.M. "Jonathan!" she called softly. He smiled in his sleep before rolling over on the sofa, his back to her.

Stephanie got up and threw her book on the chair. Turning away from Jonathan, she marched over to the window. Moonlight danced on the snow, while bright clouds sailed across the sky. What a romantic night, not that Jonathan could stay up long enough to notice, she thought, a sour taste in her mouth. She felt angry and annoyed at Jonathan.

Within a second, however, she wanted to kick herself. Jonathan had every right to be tired. He, too, had worked all day. Then he'd cooked dinner *and* done the dishes, just so Stephanie could study.

The music from next door grew louder. Stephanie started tapping her feet and was soon dancing around the small apartment, half hoping Jonathan would wake up.

She began making up crazy dance steps, shaking her hair down over her face, swinging her arms. She danced around the sofa, giggling softly, and shimmied in front of Jonathan. But nothing was going to wake this man up. "Hey, turn it down, guys, it's a weeknight!" someone yelled from downstairs, banging on the pipes. The music faded.

Stephanie flopped back in her chair and twirled a strand of hair around one well-manicured finger.

Dancing by herself like this had reminded her of being back in Suite 301, Thayer Hall. One Saturday night, she, Casey, and Nancy had all converged on the common room around midnight. Casey, in a great mood, had put on some dance music. Nancy, Casey, and

Stephanie had danced and danced and danced until they were exhausted.

Finally they had collapsed into the sagging old sofa, laughing and telling one another silly, embarrassing secrets. They compared notes on what it was like the first time they had ever been kissed.

Usually Stephanie had scorned what she called "group gab sessions," but right about now she could sure use one. She wondered what her suitemates were up to. She doubted anyone there was asleep.

She had heard that Casey's new roommate was some mysterious Russian who was actually dating Nancy's ex, Jake. Stephanie didn't love Nancy but she sure felt sorry for her. That must be nasty, Stephanie thought. Certainly something to check out in person, she decided.

Being married didn't have to mean losing track of your friends. No way. A bright thought struck her and Stephanie's restless mood began to lift. Tomorrow she would head over to Thayer right before dinner to check out the scene and catch up with her old suitemates.

She hadn't seen them since her wedding. They were probably dying to hear all about the joys of married life. Hey, maybe she could show them firsthand how happy she and Jonathan were. She'd throw a housewarming party and invite everyone.

CHAPTER 3

On Tuesday morning Nancy trudged up the steps to the *Wilder Times* office, knowing there must be some country and western song to match her mood. Except she wasn't sure which mood to match—annoyed or nervous.

She was definitely annoyed at Gail for shooting down her TA article. Plus she didn't feel like sitting through a meeting with Jake, when she knew Nadia hadn't come back to the suite the night before.

Nancy sighed. The thought of another *Wilder Times* staff meeting seemed about as exciting as a lit. crit. midterm exam.

Pulling off her earmuffs, Nancy tucked them in the pocket of her coat and stopped to check the bulletin board outside the *Times* office. She scanned the usual notices:

Roommate wanted, female, nonsmoking, vegetarian, cute apartment within walking distance of campus.

Two bus tickets half price to Wilder U./ Emerson Hoops Showdown, Saturday the 18th.

Headlines: Calling All TV Wannabes!

WWST, Weston's premier cable news station, is launching a new hour of college television news. The weekly show, *Headlines,* will be produced, written, and presented by an all-student staff under the supervision of Wilder University's Media Department. WWST will donate all studio space, airtime, equipment, and technical help. Contact either Professor Isabel Ramirez or Professor Sidney Trenton in the Wilder U. Media Center to set up appointments for auditions.

Is this for real? Nancy wondered. She reread the bright yellow flyer quickly, her smile widening with every word. A cable TV station was devoting an hour of broadcast time to a college news show. Now, that was exciting.

Voices from the *Wilder Times* office spilled out into the hall. The meeting was about to start. Nancy heard Jake laughing and Gail barking orders. What if she stopped taking orders from Gail? What if she didn't need permission to check out leads? What if she had the freedom to develop her own ideas? *Headlines* might be just the ticket.

A break from Jake wouldn't hurt either. Here was her chance to get some distance from him without jeopardizing her own dreams of becoming a journalist. The tryouts for *Headlines* couldn't have come at a better time.

Nancy jotted down the professors' names and their extensions, then gasped. "I don't believe this!" she murmured, her heart sinking. The auditions at WWST were scheduled for Thursday. But to get an audition you had to have an interview, and the deadline for interviews was today, at noon. Just forty minutes from now. Nancy chewed the end of her pencil. She heard Gail call the staff meeting to order.

Nancy barely hesitated before turning and flying down the stairs straight for the nearest campus phone.

Sunlight streamed through a crack in the curtains in Room 214, Jamison Hall, and onto Bess Marvin's bed. "Ooooh!" Bess moaned, pulling the covers over her head. "Get that light outta my eyes!" she cried out loud. She opened one eye and sighed. Her roommate, Leslie King, had left for classes, probably ages ago. Bess had the room to herself.

Her temples were pounding. Her mouth tasted as if she'd spent the night chewing on an old wool sock. The lead weight in the middle of her stomach felt as if she had swallowed a shoe, whole.

This is exactly what a hangover is supposed to feel like, she thought. Except all she'd had to drink the night before was water, black coffee, and more water. But she had eaten . . . and eaten . . . and eaten. Bess groaned softly and opened her other eye. She was lying face-down on her bed. Under the covers she felt something cardboardy. She lifted the blanket and saw an open shoe box. Inside were three plastic Baggies from the Cave, several crumpled candy wrappers, a peanut butter cup and three mint patties—still unopened—and half a bag of pretzels. That's all that was left of her emergency snack stash. How come no one ever talked about food hangovers? She glanced over at her digital alarm—11:45 A.M.

"No!" she wailed. Twenty minutes to make it to her class, and the professor had told her to stop cutting. Bess sat up quickly. The room swirled around her and her stomach clutched in a terrible cramp. "I'm going to be sick!"

A little while later, after a shower, Bess stood in front of her mirror, feeling much better, but incredibly embarrassed. After all her hard dieting, she had really blown it. She would be sure to burst her slip at the seams. You look awful! Bess told the pasty face that looked back at her from the mirror. And fat! Bess forced herself to take a good hard look at herself in her bra and panties. She pinched the flesh around her waist. More than yesterday morning, that was for sure.

She grabbed the wrappers from her pig-out of the night before, crumpled them as small as she could, and tossed them into the wastepaper basket. Putting the cover back on the shoe box, she shoved it way under her bed, where it would be hard to reach.

Bess pursed her lips and slipped into an oversize gray sweater and baggy jeans. She took a deep breath. Well, she couldn't erase what happened last night. She had blown her diet, lost control. That was that. But—she smiled wanly—today was a brand-new day and the calorie slate was empty. Bess was determined to keep it that way.

"Nancy Drew, television journalist." Nancy tried on the new identity as she dashed through the double glass doors of Wilder University's Media Center.

She crossed the atrium and hurried down the hall toward Isabel Ramirez's office.

After setting up her appointment with Professor Ramirez on the phone, Nancy had rushed back to her room to pick up her portfolio. She could only hope that her print clippings from the *Wilder Times* would show her promise as a broadcast news journalist. As she raced back out, however, it dawned on her that a sweatshirt and jeans *didn't* show promise at all. Her brown gabardine pants were pressed and her maroon silk blouse had been freshly dry-cleaned. She left Thayer Hall in record time, looking very professional.

The campus clock struck twelve noon as Nancy knocked confidently on the door.

"Come in," a woman's voice beckoned.

The small office was cozy and welcoming. A woman, maybe thirty or so, glanced up from watering an exotic fern on the window sill.

"Professor Ramirez?" Nancy asked.

"Yes, and you must be Nancy Drew," the professor said in a warm, deep voice. "Come on in and take a seat." She motioned Nancy to one of two overstuffed easy chairs in front of a coffee table.

"I was just about to have some tea," Professor Ramirez said. "Would you like some?"

"Sure," Nancy said. As she sat down, Nancy cast her journalist's eye on the professor pouring the tea. Isabel Ramirez had large, almond-shaped dark eyes and thick black hair tied back in a sophisticated twist. She was smartly dressed in a black pantsuit that showed off her slim figure to advantage.

The professor handed Nancy a mug of tea and sat down in the other chair. She took a sip from her own cup before speaking. "So, you would like to audition for *Headlines.*"

"Definitely," Nancy said. "It sounds like the perfect opportunity to learn about broadcast journalism."

"Yes, quite an opportunity, for the right student," the professor replied. "But before I tell you more about the show, Nancy, tell me about yourself. You mentioned that you are a reporter for the *Wilder Times.*"

"Yes, I am." Nancy paused to organize her thoughts. "I'm a journalism major, and I joined the paper as soon as I came to Wilder in September."

Professor Ramirez frowned. "You're only a freshman?"

"But I have lots of experience already on the paper. Here are some articles with my by-line." She handed the professor the black loose-leaf binder that held samples of her writing.

The professor's face seemed neutral, until she looked up from the book. She smiled broadly. "I'm impressed, Nancy. Your work shows promise. You are a very talented journalist . . . and very mature for a freshman."

Nancy beamed. "Thank you."

"But why do you want to leave the *Times?* You seem to be doing well for yourself there."

Nancy had tried to prepare herself for this question. "Because," she said sincerely, "I feel I could be—no, I *should* be—doing more."

"More? More what?"

"I need more independence," Nancy answered instantly.

Professor Ramirez sat back in her chair, sipping her tea a moment. Then she laughed. "I think you might be just the person we're looking for at *Headlines.*"

"You mean that?" Nancy exclaimed, thrilled.

"I do. I will certainly set up an audition for you on Thursday—if you want it."

"Want it?" Nancy laughed. "Oh, yes."

Professor Ramirez held up a hand, palm out. "I know a bit about you, but you know nothing about our plans—or lack of plans as the case may be. You'll need to know what we're doing to decide.

"When WWST came up with the idea of a weekly college hour, they wanted us to find a student who's savvy in journalism, plus has a pulse on what's hot on campus socially, academically, politically. It's a chance to build something from the ground up, to design the program, balancing hard news with feature stories."

"This sounds too good to be true!" Nancy

exclaimed. "You mean that this person, this student, would be in charge?"

Isabel Ramirez laughed. "Well, there will be a station manager to make sure nothing gets out of hand, and everything will have to be okayed by either Professor Trenton or myself. If you get the job, you'll also have to learn the nuts and bolts of TV news reporting, everything from camera work and filming interviews to editing videotape. But I don't want to scare you with the technical part. WWST's deal is that they will provide technical equipment, training, and expertise. It's like an apprenticeship for Wilder students."

"So other students will be on board?" Nancy asked.

The professor nodded. "Oh, yes, a small staff, a crew. But the structure and production of the show itself would be your job. We are only auditioning for the top position now. So, what do you think, Nancy. Still interested?"

"Are you kidding? A chance to be in charge of my own show?" Nancy blurted out, and instantly cringed. Talk about sounding like a freshman.

"So that's a yes?" Professor Ramirez smiled broadly at Nancy and stood up. "The schedule is booked, but I'll squeeze in an audition for you." She checked the calendar on her desk. "How's Thursday afternoon?"

"Fine, just fine," replied Nancy.

Walking back to her dorm, Nancy mused on her day. Only that morning, she had been dreading the *Wilder Times* meeting. Now she had stumbled on the chance to run her own TV show and never have to attend another *Times* meeting again.

Before Nancy knew it, she was on the steps of her dorm. First things first, she told herself. Nancy needed to make sure that no one, absolutely no one, came between her and her new dream. She had less than two days to learn all she could about running a TV show.

CHAPTER 4

Close your eyes, Jake, and keep them closed until I tell you to open," Nadia called from the kitchen of Jake's apartment.

"What happens if I open them?"

"You spoil my surprise dessert."

The disappointment in Nadia's voice made Jake's heart melt. "Not to worry. I won't even peep."

"You are a good boy, Jake Collins. I like good American boys."

"Is that supposed to be a compliment?" Jake laughed. No one had ever called him good before. He thought of himself as a decent person, but more as a tough guy with a nose for news than a good American boy.

Nadia laughed a knowing laugh. "Yes. Yet

I do not mean you are too good. I like to think inside *everyone* there is a naughty part, too."

"Inside you, too?" Jake mocked slightly.

"Of course! I am surprised you have not noticed this yet about me," Nadia said. "Now, quiet. I need to concentrate on the *pièce de résistance.*"

Jake obediently kept his eyes closed. He was afraid if he opened them, their whole evening together would prove to have been just a dream. Nadia had spent hours and incredible energy cooking him the best meal he had eaten since coming to college. Every dish was delicate, exotic, and, Nadia swore, purely Russian.

Nancy had never cooked for him.

Maybe an independent, nonhomebody type like Nancy was what he needed as a friend, but maybe he needed a girlfriend who pampered him from time to time.

Jake grinned, then sniffed the air. "You sure you're not burning the house down?"

"Not the house, no." Nadia chuckled, her voice sounding nearer. "But you smell right. Something *is* burning." He heard Nadia set a plate down on the table. He felt heat rising to his face and smelled something sweet and delicious. He inhaled more deeply, and smelled something even sweeter and more delicious: Iris at Midnight, Nadia's perfume. Like her, it was beautiful, exotic, and dusky.

Jake sensed Nadia's presence behind his

chair and then felt the palms of her warm hands seal his eyes. He reached up and touched her wrists. Her skin was soft as rose petals. He ran his hands up the wide silky sleeves of her shirt.

"Later, Jake," Nadia whispered into his ear. "But, now," she commanded in a louder voice, removing her hands, "open. Right away. Before it is too late!"

Jake opened his eyes. The center of the table seemed to be on fire. "Wow! You really are going to burn the house down."

"Never!" Nadia swung around to face Jake. Her smile was dazzling. "Do you like? See, the outside only makes the fire. I pour brandy all over the outside, and it makes pretty flames! Inside it is all cold. Fire and ice, like me!"

Jake was well aware of Nadia's fire, but doubted the ice part. "I had this as a kid! It's got ice cream inside, right? But it doesn't melt in the oven."

Nadia nodded. "A magic dessert. I call it Karloff Flambé." Nadia laughed and sat down across from Jake. A moment later the flames subsided.

"What is so Russian about this?" Jake pretended to look offended. "Looks like baked Alaska to me! And Alaska, last I heard, was the forty-ninth state, which makes it part of my country."

Nadia's beautifully shaped eyebrows arched.

"Alaska, yes. That you imperialist Americans bought from us Russians when we were too naive to know the value. I think of Alaska as part of my homeland."

Afraid that he'd offended her, Jake touched the back of her hand. She shivered with pleasure. He sought her eyes and said, "So Alaska is something else we have in common." Jake watched as Nadia began to slice through the thick toasted meringue topping.

"You're amazing," Jake said, after tasting the first bite.

Nadia smiled in the glow of the candles that romantically adorned the little table. Her eyes, gleaming with the reflection of the flames, were moist with tears.

"Forgive me," she said, a catch in her voice. "I sometimes think I am too emotional, like a Russian, to be with an American man like you."

Jake got up and crossed over to her side of the table and drew her up out of her chair. "Nadia Karloff," he said, choking up too, "what I adore about you is just that. No holds barred. What you see is what you get!"

Nadia's cheeks, already burnished by the flames of the dessert and the candles, colored more deeply. "Jake, I do not understand holding bars and—"

"Never mind," Jake said, and led her over to the couch. He sat down, guiding her next to him. He cupped her face in his hands. "Nadia," he said, losing himself in her eyes, "I just meant that you are open and let all your feelings show. When you are sad, happy, when you want to kiss, when you are angry—you aren't afraid to let it all show. You are always honest."

"You are such a sweet man!" she said.

"Sweet?" Jake leaned back from her.

"I say the word wrong?" Nadia asked.

"No. It's just that, well, first I'm good and now I'm *sweet!*" Jake looked at Nadia quizzically. "What makes me sweet, besides too much of your dessert?"

"One can never eat too much of Karloff Flambé." Nadia laughed softly. "No, I just think how you are kind, and perhaps a little naive. . . ." Nadia shrugged. "Ah, why try to explain away the mystery?" she whispered, snuggling up close to him, and lifting her lips to his.

Exactly, Jake thought to himself as he covered her lips with his own. She lay back on the couch and he lowered himself over her, and, again, searched out her lips.

"Jake," Nadia gasped a few minutes later, pushing him away.

Jake raised himself up slightly, the world out of focus, his heart pounding. "Is something wrong?" he asked.

"Wrong?" Nadia searched his face intently.

"No, not wrong. It is only . . . only that I feel so much here." She took his hand and pressed it to her heart. "I can barely stand it."

Jake drank her in, dazzled. "Man, I can't believe this."

"You—you do not feel the same way?" Nadia's voice faltered.

Jake gently guided her hand over his heart. "Nadia, I feel very much the same way."

Nadia's expression softened. She lowered her eyes. "I try to pretend it is not so, but I am falling in love with you, Jake Collins."

Jake sat back on his heels and pulled Nadia up into his arms. "Nadia," he whispered, running his hand through her rumpled hair. As revelation dawned on him, he said, "I told myself this could not be happening. It's too fast. I'm on the rebound from Nancy. But Nadia, I'm not. *This* is the truth, the real thing. I'm in love with you." Feeling purely happy, Jake started to laugh.

Nadia began to giggle, her white teeth glittering between her quivering lips. "It is wonderful, no? I thought love would make me feel sad. But with you I feel happy, yes?"

"Me, too!" Jake said. He couldn't believe his incredible luck. Here, this stunning, exotic woman, this Nadia, was not only interested in him, but loved him.

Jake had always felt that, deep down, he harbored something special inside, something that might appeal to a very special woman. But he had figured all the other guys probably felt the same way. Nadia's choice of him, above all these other guys, confirmed his belief in himself.

Nancy hadn't swept Jake away like this. Nadia was a tidal wave of passion. She was moonlight, changeable and elusive, but at the same time, she was as intoxicating as the sun on a hot summer day. "This is exactly how love should be," he whispered.

Nadia leaned back against Jake, wrapping his arms around her waist. "You know, Jake, when I was a little girl in Moscow I imagined being in love someday. Girls do that, you know," she said, looking up at him, a playful expression in her eyes.

"Little boys don't," Jake said. "I never imagined love. I imagined being a hero."

"Russian men the same. But I think I picture you as a wonderful father someday."

"A father?" Jake's mouth fell open. He had never pictured that scene.

"Not now, silly man." Nadia rapped him lightly on the back of his hands. "But someday. You are the kind of person who will be good to share a life with someday." Closing her eyes, Nadia nestled in the crook of his arm.

Jake felt flattered and confused all at once. He looked down at her. With her eyes closed, her thick, long, dark lashes brushed the tops of her high cheekbones. He would never get tired of looking at that face, of touching her, of talking to her. Suddenly he wondered what it would be like sharing day-to-day life with this amazing woman.

Nadia Karloff Collins. The name crossed Jake's mind. His throat went dry. Now, that would be a big step, a giant step. But when he was ready, someday after graduation, maybe Nadia would be there to take it with him.

"I'm ba—ack!" Stephanie announced from the door to Suite 301, Thayer Hall, Tuesday night. Kara Verbeck, Casey Fontaine, and Ginny Yuen were in the common room with two boxes of pizza open on the coffee table. Stephanie hadn't had take-out pizza in ages.

"What? Divorced already?" Kara asked, feigning shock.

Stephanie's heart sank. "Glad to see you, too!" she snapped.

"Stephanie, she's only kidding," Casey said, jumping up and hugging her. "How've you been?"

"More to the point—how's married life?" Ginny looked up from the floor where she was stretching.

Stephanie tossed her dark brown cashmere coat on the back of the couch and plunked herself down next to Casey. "Married life is, well, great. Just great!" she said, smiling at Ginny, Casey, and Kara in turn. She was about to say more, when she heard voices coming from Nancy's room.

"Hey, Nancy, guess who's here?" Casey shouted. "Stephanie Keats—I mean Baur!"

"Either will do," Stephanie said, blushing slightly. "It's hard to get used to a new name after eighteen years of your old one."

Nancy walked into the common room, followed by her friend George Fayne. "Hi, Stephanie, good to see you!" Nancy said warmly. Stephanie eyed Nancy carefully. Nancy looked pretty terrific. Certainly not like a woman with a broken heart.

"Did Jonathan set you free for the evening?" George remarked, throwing her lanky body on the floor next to Ginny and snagging one of the two remaining slices of pizza.

"I don't need Jonathan's permission to visit my friends!" Stephanie replied tartly, wondering how Nancy put up with George. "Besides, you sound like you think marriage is some kind of prison."

"If it is, it sure suits you," Ginny said.

Stephanie gawked at Ginny. "Really?" She'd been thinking she was looking a bit pale lately.

"What's it like, Stephanie?" Nancy asked, settling down next to George. "Is it what you expected?"

Stephanie forced a laugh. "Not at all." She let her words hang expectantly in the air, then grinned. "Better." Everyone cracked up. "I mean, he even cooks for me," she bragged, encouraged by her friends' response.

"That's worth writing home about!" Casey remarked.

"Will whips up a mighty impressive bowl of microwave popcorn," George said.

"Hey, I'm not talking popcorn!" Stephanie informed them. "I'm talking Italian gourmet!" Actually, she was sick of Jonathan's spaghetti drowning in thick canned tomato sauce, though she'd die before she'd admit it to anyone.

"Sounds like marriage has uncovered aspects of Jonathan you never even suspected!" Nancy teased.

"Any horrible dark secrets?" Kara inquired.

"Or wonderful surprises?" Ginny asked.

"No, Kara. You bet, Ginny. But I'm not talking," Stephanie demurred, hoping no one would guess that most nights meant TV or studying rather than romance.

"So you recommend the married state?" Casey asked. "Maybe Charley and I shouldn't wait for graduation."

"Makes me think you and Will shouldn't either," Kara teased George.

George gasped. "No way! I love Will Blackfeather, but I don't intend to get married anytime soon—to Will, or anyone else."

"You've got to admit, you guys are more than serious," Ginny remarked.

"Sure, but serious doesn't always mean wedding bells," George said firmly.

"And being happy doesn't mean you have to rush to the altar either," Nancy said.

"Maybe marrying in college isn't for everyone," Stephanie conceded. Maybe not even for me, she added silently to herself.

"Maybe not marriage, but love is!" Kara laughed. "Or at least it's in the air around here."

"Love?" Stephanie leaned forward. "Here?"

"Looks that way." Casey chuckled. "If Nadia Karloff moves out, the housing service should use that angle to advertise for my next roommate. 'Room Two A in Three-oh-one, hot line to love!' "

"Now this is news." Stephanie feigned ignorance. "Who's the guy?" She glanced at Nancy out of the corner of her eye.

"Would you believe it?" Nancy answered with a wry grin. "It's Jake."

"You're kidding," Stephanie said, full of fake surprise. "Not your Jake."

"Not mine anymore. Not for a while now," Nancy said calmly, which Stephanie found maddening.

"So, Nadia is in love with Jake Collins. Things sure move fast around here," Stephanie said.

46

Everyone laughed.

"That's putting it mildly," Casey said.

"She must really be something to get Jake over you, Nancy," Stephanie remarked, trying to get a rise out of Nancy.

"I'll take that as a compliment," Nancy shot back at Stephanie.

"You sound a tiny bit irritated, Nancy." Stephanie smiled, sure she'd caught something like jealousy in Nancy's voice.

"Irritated?" Nancy shrugged. "Nadia's interesting and more than beautiful. I'm glad Jake's met her. But he *is* moving fast."

"Or maybe *she* is," Stephanie suggested.

"That's a novel idea," George said. "Nadia seems more like the shy type to me."

Casey nodded vigorously. "She doesn't seem to have made many other friends yet, besides Jake."

"Language problems?" Stephanie asked.

"Nadia's English is good," Ginny said.

"I think she really is shy," Nancy continued. "Her father's a poet back in Russia. She seems a little homesick and calls home a lot."

"She's opened up some since we first met her. Not that she's around much," Kara commented. "Jake's probably good for her."

"I wonder if I've ever seen her around," Stephanie mused.

"You'd remember her if you'd met her. She's dark-haired, with fine features, and incredibly beautiful skin," Casey said, scrambling to her feet and going into her room. A moment later she returned with a photo in her hand. "I don't think Nadia would mind if I showed you this." She handed Stephanie a snapshot of Nadia, hugging a tall young man.

"I know her!" Stephanie exclaimed instantly. "She sure raised some eyebrows this weekend in Berrigan's."

"How so?" Nancy asked.

"She bought two dozen pairs of designer jeans on sale. The buyer in the junior sportswear department freaked. Nadia nearly bought out the stock. Oh, and she used cash!" Stephanie studied the photo. "Every guy's head turned when she passed. I think I like her."

"I was here all day Saturday," Kara remarked. "Nadia came in with Jake, but I don't remember any shopping bags."

"I haven't seen her wearing any new clothes," Casey said, surprised. "And she hardly ever wears jeans."

"Yeah, she usually wears leggings and short skirts," Ginny said.

"And those leather pants!" Kara and Nancy chimed in.

"They fit like gloves. But hey, if I could pull it off, I'd wear them, too," Casey said.

"Well, unless Nadia's got a double, this is the woman who bought all the stuff Saturday."

"Seriously," Nancy said. "Nobody buys

Nancy wasn't listening. "Have you looked at this photo carefully?"

"Why, Nan?" George asked, becoming serious. "What did you find?"

"See how dressed up Nadia is?"

Ginny laughed. "When isn't Nadia dressed up?"

"Not like this." Nancy passed the photo around. Each of the girls took a closer look.

"I still don't get it," Kara said. "So, she's wearing a long white sun dress. It doesn't look like much, if you want my opinion."

"Maybe not, but the man is wearing a suit," Nancy said.

"Nancy, is there a point to all this? So, they were going out someplace nice for dinner."

"No, they weren't. At least not at the moment this was taken." Nancy took the photo back and pointed to a monument in the background. "That's a World War Two memorial. Brides in Russia traditionally leave their bouquets at war monuments after the wedding. See? Nadia's holding flowers."

"What are you saying? That Nadia is married to this guy?" Kara asked incredulously. "She told us she doesn't even have a boyfriend back home."

"I can't see Nadia getting married in a sun dress," Casey said. "Besides, look at all the other people in the background. They look like they're out for a day in the park."

"The flowers could be from anywhere," Ginny said. "But, now that you mention it, she does look a little like a bride."

"Nancy, as your good friend," began George, in her best imitation of Sigmund Freud, "I must tell you that you are reading too much into this photo. It is disturbing your mind. Now hand it over."

Everyone laughed, including Nancy. She passed the photo to George, who passed it on to Casey, who put it back where she had gotten it. Only Nancy noticed that the back of the photo had a line of red-pen hearts drawn along its edges like a border. Inside the border were two names in Russian, with a heart drawn between them.

I wonder if Jake knows about Nadia's brother, or her shopping spree, or all her calls to Russia, Nancy wondered.

Bess lay in the dark staring up at her ceiling, wondering how fashion models survived staying so thin. True to her word, she had not eaten a thing all day. She had drunk four bottles of spring water and allowed herself one calorie—a diet soda.

But her stomach was feeling as bad as it did when she stuffed it with junk.

She rolled over on her side, clutched her stomach, and tried not to listen to her roommate Leslie's peaceful breathing in the bed next to hers.

At least the coast was clear, Bess thought. Clear for what? Bess could picture the shoe box beneath her bed. Her emergency food stash. What was left after last night's raid? Instantly she began to take mental inventory. One bag of pretzels, three mint patties, and a peanut butter cup.

It wasn't much, but it was enough to make her mouth begin to water. Suddenly Bess was on the floor, reaching far under her bed to get her hands on the box. She climbed back into bed with her treasures. She quietly lifted off the lid and groped around inside.

Her fingers closed on the bag of pretzels. The paper crackled loud enough to wake the dead. Bess stopped and held her own breath while listening for Leslie's. She determined that her roommate was still asleep.

Bess had forgotten she'd already eaten half of the pretzels the night before. "Just one," she thought, "to take the edge off my appetite. To settle my stomach." She bit into the pretzel. The crunch was deafening, but Leslie hadn't stirred. Two minutes later she'd finished the rest of the bag. A minute after that she had stuffed her mouth with the first of her mint patties, then the second, and finally the third.

She unwrapped the peanut butter cup and popped it in her mouth. The shoe box was empty. Bess felt herself growing fatter and fatter by the second. She waited for her stomach to revolt as it had before, but it was placidly digesting. Now what, she wondered. Then she remembered having heard someone in Kappa house say, "If you eat too much, just *make* yourself throw up. You won't get fat that way. I do it all the time."

That was the answer!

When Bess came back from the bathroom a few minutes later, her knees were shaking and she was in a cold sweat. Worse than that, the lights were on and Leslie was up.

"Bess?" Leslie swept her long light brown hair off her face. Regarding Bess with sleepy green eyes, she asked, "Are you okay?"

"I'm fine," Bess answered quickly, though she felt pretty awful, both mentally and physically.

"Are you sure?"

Something in Leslie's voice made Bess straighten right up.

"Of course I'm sure," Bess snapped. She was definitely not in the mood for one of Leslie's lectures. Her roommate had loosened up a lot since they first met in September, but sometimes the girl didn't know how to bend the rules.

"It's two o'clock in the morning, Bess. You look a little green. Is your stomach bothering you"—Leslie hesitated ever so slightly—"again?"

"Give me a break, Leslie. Can't a person use the bathroom in the middle of the night without her roommate commenting on it?"

"Bess . . . oh, never mind," Leslie said, throwing herself back down on her bed, and flicking out the light.

"Good night," she said to Bess, before rolling over.

"Same to you," Bess grumbled, and wove her way back to bed, feeling anything but good. How in the world would she get through the next day feeling like a truck had just run over her?

CHAPTER 5

Nancy walked into Gail Gardeski's office first thing the next morning with mixed emotions. "Got a minute?" she asked.

Gail glanced up from the daily paper she was reading and cracked a small smile at Nancy. "Sure. The look on your face says you're onto another lead for a story. When you missed the staff meeting yesterday, I figured you were out investigating. I'm ready to listen." Gail leaned back in her chair, motioning for Nancy to sit down.

Nancy sat on the edge of the seat. "I need a leave of absence from the paper. Maybe permanently."

Gail's jaw dropped. "What? Why? What happened?"

"Nothing's happened—or not yet, but Wilder U and Weston's cable station are putting together a college-run news show—"

"*Headlines.* Yes, Professors Trenton and Ramirez's new Media Department project."

"Yesterday I interviewed with Professor Ramirez. I've decided to audition for the job of running the show," Nancy stated bluntly. "Professor Ramirez was pretty encouraging about my chances. I won't have time for the paper and the TV program."

Gail regarded Nancy with disappointment. "Nancy, you're smart enough to make your own decisions, but I'd hate to lose you. You're one of the two best reporters I've got. When you're a senior you'll probably have my job."

Nancy had thought about becoming editor-in-chief, but she was surprised to hear it from Gail, who had at times been supportive but at other times treated her like a Mouseketeer. "Thanks for your vote of confidence. But I feel like I'm running in place here—lots of work and getting nowhere. Senior year is a long time off to wait to be in charge of something."

Gail studied Nancy carefully. "Does this have anything to do with our last meeting, and my telling you no go on the TA article?"

Nancy frowned. "Your decision just gave me the push I needed. When I saw the announcement for the audition, I realized it was time to make a change."

"What if I told you you could fly with your story? Would that change your mind?"

"No. Not at all." Nancy was sure of that.

"You won't reconsider, Nancy?" Gail asked. "You may not get the TV job. . . ."

"No," Nancy stated, amazed that Gail was trying so hard to sway her from leaving. Maybe Gail valued her more than Nancy had recognized. Nancy started to wonder if she would regret her decision. "Not that I won't miss this place," she added quietly, and pushed back her chair to stand.

Gail got up and shook Nancy's hand. "Good luck, Nancy. I wish I could change your mind, but I see I can't. The door is always open if you decide you want to come back."

Nancy headed toward her cubicle. Sadness crept over her as she cleared out her desk drawers. She'd had a lot of fun, interesting, and exciting experiences working for the paper. She began to get a little nervous. Had she jumped the gun here? What if she didn't land the job at *Headlines?*

You'll live, a voice inside prompted. Gail said the door to the *Wilder Times* would always be open for you. Nancy's sadness and nervousness were soon eclipsed by mounting excitement. Nancy had a good feeling about her audition. She quickly finished packing up her things, grabbed her coat, and headed out the door.

"Whoa!" Strong hands grabbed her arms as

she stepped into the hall without looking where she was going.

"Sorry!" Nancy apologized. "Oh, Jake!" she exclaimed happily. "Am I glad to see you!" Maybe now that they wouldn't be working together, they really could be friends.

"Same here." Jake's smile seemed to stretch from ear to ear.

Nancy couldn't help but stare. She hadn't seen Jake in such a purely good mood since, since . . . when? Since the night she had confessed to him how much she loved him. That night, he had had the same glow. Nancy cleared her throat, swallowing the memory.

Jake was leaning back against the wall, regarding her with frank curiosity. "What's up, Nan? You look like you've got news."

"Am I that easy to read?" Nancy laughed, quickly regaining her poise. "You might as well be the first to know. I've decided to quit the paper."

Jake's smile vanished. "No way!"

"There's more to life than the *Wilder Times*," Nancy stated.

"No one said there wasn't, but isn't this a little sudden?"

Nancy shrugged. "Yes, it's *very* sudden. I've decided to try my hand at broadcast journalism. WSTN is co-sponsoring a college TV show, and I'm auditioning to run it."

Jake was unimpressed. "Nancy, it's not like

you to walk out on a commitment just because a little more glamour comes along."

"Jake, this has nothing to do with glamour," Nancy said, beginning to get annoyed. "It's a great opportunity, and if I get it I'm going to take it."

"You sure it's about opportunity and not about—us?"

Nancy was definitely annoyed now. "Look, Jake, everything in my life doesn't revolve around 'us.' In fact, there *is* no *'us.'* "

"Look, Nan, I know it's hard working together. But given a little time . . . when you meet . . ."

"Jake, would you just shut up and listen?" Nancy cried hotly. "This is *my* decision. It has to do with what *I* want to explore for my future. My world does not revolve around *you.*"

Jake threw up his hands. "Sorry I mentioned it. Good luck," he said, and brushed past Nancy and strode into the newspaper office.

Nancy glared after him, then turned and marched down the hall, heading for the stairs. Where did men get such humongous egos?

As Stephanie wriggled into her Silky Elegance stockings, she stared in despair at her living room. Earlier she had moved the lamp from one side of the sofa to the other. Did the room look better now? Or worse?

"Only you could look beautiful like this."

Jonathan came up from behind and wrapped himself around her.

"Jonathan," Stephanie said, squirming away. "You'll snag my stockings!" She smoothed the faux silk over her legs. "Maybe we should cancel this party," she said with a pout.

"And spend Saturday night alone?" Jonathan suggested. He picked up her sweater from the couch and gently pulled it over her head. His hands lingered on her waist. Stephanie fluffed her hair, and went to the closet, out of Jonathan's reach, to grab her skirt. "I could think of worse fates, you know," Jonathan concluded.

"Right, like our friends taking up a collection on the spot because we're so obviously hard up! Even the Weston thrift shop would turn down this couch."

"We are?" Jonathan blinked. "It would?"

Stephanie yanked up the zipper on her skirt. "Look at this place. It's shabby and dark. I can't believe I'm living like this."

"Hey, it's just a student apartment." Jonathan took a hard look at the room. "Maybe we could fix it up."

"By Saturday?"

"Sure." Jonathan went to the desk and pulled out the calculator. He punched in some figures. "I suppose we could invade our savings for a few things. If we budget carefully, maybe we could buy a couple of pillows or something to brighten up the place."

Stephanie stopped in the middle of putting on her high-heeled boot. She was too shocked to complain about his saying the word *budget.* "You mean we could *buy* stuff?"

"We could stretch the budget, pick up a couple of throw pillows. And, how much can a plant or two cost?"

Stephanie practically cheered. "Not much! House and Home is having a sale starting tomorrow."

"Well, I was thinking of Berrigan's, where we can use our employee discount. There's a bin of irregular pillows in Home Furnishings," Jonathan said.

Stephanie narrowed her eyes at Jonathan's suggestion, but decided not to complain. She threw her arms around his neck. "Oh, Jonathan, I'm so excited," she said. "I was beginning to dread this party. Now I won't feel so, well, thrift-shoppy." She could probably get nicer pillows at House and Home on sale for just a little more than Berrigan's old irregulars, she thought. Jonathan needn't ever know.

Jake was almost finished with his sandwich when Nadia swept into the Cave. Her broad-brimmed hat rested low over her forehead, and she clutched her cape high up on her neck. Jake couldn't see her face until she sat down next to him, keeping her back turned to the rest of the room.

"Nadia, what's wrong?" Jake exclaimed, as she slipped off her cape. Tears streamed in rivers down Nadia's cheeks.

"Oh, Jake," she cried, clutching his arm with her slender hands. "Everything is wrong. Just everything. I think maybe I am not meant ever to be happy. Ever." With that, she buried her head in her hands.

"Nadia," he said quietly, "has something happened at home? With your father or mother or . . ."

"No. My father, he is fine—I think. But no. It is my visa," she confided, pulling a tissue out of her oversize tapestry bag. She paused, struggling to master her feelings. Finally her tears slowed, and she lifted her red-rimmed eyes to look at Jake. "The administration office tells me that a problem has come up with my visa. It is good for only another six weeks and then I will be deported."

"Deported . . ." he said in a fog. A moment later the words' meaning hit Jake with the force of lightning. "You mean you have to leave?" he asked, horrified. He touched her lips with the tip of his fingers. "This can't be. There must be a mistake."

Nadia moved her chair closer to Jake. "I know. It can't be. Not now." The passion in her voice rang clearly. "But there is no mistake."

"But a student visa is supposed to be good until you graduate," protested Jake.

"That is what is supposed to be. But some problems came up in Russia—with my family. Now my visa will be revoked."

"The university must be able to do something."

Shaking her head dismally, Nadia said, "The people in the Student Affairs office were very nice, but there is nothing they can do."

"Six weeks . . ." Jake murmured. Was that all they had left together? "Isn't there anything we can do?"

"Jake, if there were, I would do anything to stay . . ." Nadia looked at him shyly. "To stay with you, I would do it."

Jake's feelings of helplessness suddenly turned into a reporter's determination. "I'll find out what we need to do. I'm an investigative reporter, after all."

"Oh, no, Jake. There is nothing you can do. Nothing at all. I have called Immigration. They were not as nice as at the university, but a woman there told me what would be necessary. Unless I was marrying a citizen, I will have to get on a plane to leave America."

"That's it? Just like that?" Jake asked.

"Laws are simple and hard," Nadia said, her lower lip quivering. "Just like that. But you can come and visit me in Russia," she said with a brave smile.

"Yeah," Jake said. "Like I could get the money to spend time in Russia."

"Maybe you would come and be an exchange student at Moscow University," Nadia suggested, trying to smile.

Her sadness on top of her beauty took Jake's breath away. Suddenly her words broke into his consciousness: marry a U.S. citizen. Jake let the idea knock around his brain for a second or two.

"Jake, be brave about this. *I* will. Love like ours, no distance will change. Ever." Nadia began to kiss him passionately and with so much urgency that Jake forgot all about visas, marriage, and the fact that the Cave was jammed with curious students eyeing them.

Nancy checked her watch as she rushed through the quad. On Wednesdays, the Media Center library was open only until 5:00 P.M., which left her very little time. Her audition was in about twenty-four hours: twenty-four hours to become an expert on the nuts and bolts of television. And twenty-four hours to learn the ins and outs of TV anchoring.

She was so engrossed in her thoughts that she almost walked right past Jake without seeing him. His head was bent so low, he couldn't see her, which tempted her to keep on walking without saying hello. The last thing she needed was another discussion like their last one. But something about Jake made her stop. The spring was gone from his step; he looked devastated.

"Hi, Jake," she said, wondering what was wrong.

He looked up blankly, then smiled faintly. "We keep running into each other."

She nodded. "I'm on my way to the Media Center before it closes," she told him.

"Your audition go okay?" he asked absently.

"Thanks for asking, but it's not until tomorrow." Nancy debated whether to ask him if everything was okay with him. He really looked as if he needed a friend. Ten minutes more or less at the library wouldn't matter. "What's up?"

"Life just threw me a curve." Jake grimaced. "Nadia's having visa problems."

"She is?" Nancy frowned, turning up the collar of her coat against the wind.

"Big time." Jake looked off into the distance. "Just now, just when . . ." Jake broke off.

"What kind of problems, Jake?"

"Her visa is being revoked. She's going to be deported."

"No way!" Nancy was stunned. "That's unbelievable. Why? Isn't there something she can do to stay? Has she spoken to an immigration lawyer?"

"I don't think so. According to her there's no point. Immigration was pretty definite about it."

Nancy touched Jake's arm. "You must feel awful, Jake. Maybe more than anyone, I can see how much you care for her. I wish there was something I could do to help."

"There isn't," Jake replied grimly. He looked into Nancy's face and his expression softened. "But I'm glad you feel that way—that you'd help if you could. I don't think there's anything anyone can do. It makes me sick. . . ." Jake choked up.

Nancy stood a moment, not knowing what to say. The campus clock struck four, and she roused herself. "Jake, I have to go before the Media Center closes."

" 'Bye," Jake mumbled as he turned and walked away.

Nancy added this news to the list of mysteries surrounding Nadia: buying two dozen pairs of jeans, all those phone calls to Russia, the photo that might be a wedding picture, and now, deportation. What was the connection? Nancy had a hunch that Nadia was hiding something, but what? She shook the thought from her mind. Nancy had to concentrate on her audition for the TV news show. She didn't have time to sort out Nadia's story. Besides, if Nadia was being deported, what difference would it make?

CHAPTER 6

Thursday afternoon Stephanie marched into House and Home, a one-day-sale flyer clutched in her gloved hand.

The delicious scent of retail and the sight of the broad aisles filled with never-been-used merchandise set her pulse racing. Stephanie believed that to get the best quality for the best price, one had to go to specialty stores, not general department stores like Berrigan's.

Not that one hundred dollars was going to go far at either store, but that was the highest Jonathan would go. A true shopper, Stephanie felt challenged to make it stretch as far as she could.

The store directory said throw pillows and something called occasional lamps were upstairs. Jonathan hadn't mentioned lamps, but Stephanie figured that pillows couldn't cost much—they were just stuffed squares of fabric, after all—surely she could squeeze one lamp out of her budget.

A display of living room furniture at the top of the escalator lured Stephanie right off course. "What harm could it do?" she murmured, as she sat down on a brocade sofa. It was a far cry from the corduroy wreck that filled half her living room. Stephanie's veteran shopper's heart lurched, however, when she checked the price tag. Even on sale, it cost half her annual, part-time salary at Berrigan's.

Stephanie knew Jonathan's new credit card lay tucked away in the wallet in her purse, but he would need a straitjacket if she came home with this!

Stephanie jumped up off the couch and marched determinedly to the pillow department. If she and Jonathan had had a real wedding, they would have gotten all sorts of lovely gifts. It her father hadn't been so mean about her marriage, she would have been able to afford a whole living room set. For a moment Stephanie almost regretted marrying Jonathan. But she'd show them all what a good decision it had been!

Feeling proud of passing up the couch, Stephanie eyed the half-priced lamps. The lovely silver standing lamp would light the living room . . .

"Half price," a voice spoke up from behind her.

Stephanie wheeled around. "Oh!" she said to a pair of dark blue eyes belonging to a tall blond salesman with mile-wide shoulders and a quizzical smile. He held Stephanie's glance a second, and she caught his message: You are something fine, lady.

"And a lovely accent to any home," the salesman said. The price tag, however, said more than a hundred dollars.

"Ummm, too . . ." She cut herself off, unable to admit she was too poor to buy it.

"Or perhaps this table lamp?" the salesman suggested, taking Stephanie's elbow and steering her in the direction of another display. His touch sent a thrill up Stephanie's spine. She knew that salespeople were never supposed to touch customers, but that made it all the more exciting. Suddenly, confusion flooded Stephanie. Wasn't she supposed to feel this thrill only with her husband?

The solid brass table lamp was even more beautiful—and expensive—than the standing lamp. "This model gives better light, and, since it's a higher-end item to begin with, you save even more money at our half-price sale."

Stephanie ran her fingers along the warm brass surface. "You're right."

"Furniture, particularly lamps and carpets, are an investment. They last forever."

"That's true," Stephanie said, brightening. "But I just got married, and we . . ."

"Have to be careful with money, I know."

He didn't sneer at her. He understood! Stephanie relaxed a little and said, "But we have all this old ratty furniture. It's just so . . . well . . . ugly." She lifted her eyes to his. "I hate ugly things."

He held her glance again and Stephanie felt the sparks fly. She felt more like her old self than she had in ages. "No, ugliness is definitely not your style," he said. "Maybe I can help you. Will you be shopping with cash or credit?"

"Credit." The word popped right out of Stephanie's mouth, even though she had already taken a hundred dollars out of the money machine. But it was obvious to her now that she couldn't get anywhere on that.

"Good. Credit gives you a certain freedom to select just the right well-coordinated items while they're available at the right price. What did you have in mind?"

"Throw pillows," Stephanie said with as much dignity as possible. Within minutes they had selected a few colorful cushions to make her apartment cozy. Before tax, they came in just under budget.

"I hesitate to mention this, with your budget

and all, but there is something I'd love to show you. It's along the lines of an investment, but, more important, it will banish dinginess forever."

"What's that?" Stephanie said, enjoying his chitchat.

"Let me show you." Again he took her arm, and again, she felt a forbidden thrill.

He took Stephanie to a corner where rows of handwoven carpets hung from tall display racks. The sight of all that splendor made her throat go dry. "These are beautiful," she said, eyeing an Oriental in shades of autumn: warm rust, gold, and flame. It was just the right size for her living room, and Stephanie knew it would turn the dilapidated couch into shabby-chic.

"It's only six hundred dollars on sale."

"What!" Stephanie yanked her hand away, as if she'd been burned.

"On our easy payment plan, that's only forty dollars a month."

"Forty a month?" That was nothing, though at the moment she couldn't quite figure out the arithmetic. A few extra work hours at Berrigan's should cover it. "An investment," Stephanie mused out loud.

"For life."

"I'll take it. And the pillows, and, oh"—should she?—"the brass lamp."

"A magnificent ensemble!" proclaimed the salesman.

Stephanie pulled out Jonathan's brand-new credit card, feeling quite proud of her bargain hunting. She had actually saved them hundreds and hundreds of dollars.

"Now let's see," the salesman said. "How would two weeks from today be for delivery?"

"Two weeks!" Stephanie gasped. "That's awful. I need it all by Saturday or there's no point."

He frowned charmingly and scratched his head. "Let me see what I can do for you," he said, picking up the phone.

Stephanie looked at him out of the corner of her eye. Definitely a first-class hunk. He was still watching her. Stephanie preened a little and flashed him one of her more seductive smiles.

He smiled back.

Stop flirting, Keats, Stephanie told herself sternly. Lighten up, she retorted. Being married doesn't mean being dead. If a guy enjoys looking you over, and you enjoy checking him out, no harm's done. It's just good, healthy flirting.

"We're in luck uh . . . Mrs. Baur."

"Ms. will do," Stephanie said coyly and coolly. "I will have my delivery Saturday morning?"

"Better. How about by tomorrow after-

73

noon? Say after three P.M. Will someone be home?"

Stephanie's cool vanished. She almost hugged him. "Are you kidding? Wild horses couldn't drag me away!"

Jake prowled the small kitchen of his apartment, feeling like a trapped animal. He was in a no-win situation with Nadia, and he hated not winning more than anything. "Do you believe this, DiMartini?" he asked his roommate. "I don't know one guy on campus who has as much bad luck with women as I do."

"Come off it, Jake," Nick DiMartini scoffed. "Most of us haven't got half the luck you've had this year alone. First, a number-one class act like Nancy Drew."

"Right, but where did that get me? She dropped me, pure and simple. Not that I care so much about all that now. But Nadia—"

"Nadia? She's a killer!"

"You can say that again," Jake interrupted, wondering again how such a perfect woman could vanish from his life.

"Maybe if you'd stop pacing long enough to tell me what's going on I'd have more sympathy." Nick slugged some milk from the carton in his hand. "Don't tell me she's gone and dropped you, too."

Jake pressed his palms to his temples. "No. That's not it. I think maybe I could actually live through that. But this . . ." Jake took a deep breath. "Right, I keep forgetting you don't have a clue what's happened. It's gone down so fast." Jake grabbed a chair, and straddled it. "Nadia's being booted out of the country."

"You're putting me on!" Nick blurted out.

"Right—like I'd make something like that up," Jake shot back.

"By whom? When? Why?" Nick asked incredulously.

Propping his chin on his hands, Jake told Nick about Nadia's visa problems.

"That stinks," Nick exclaimed as soon as Jake finished.

"My sentiments, exactly."

"A cousin of mine had to leave the country because his family got into some sort of major legal trouble back in Italy. His visa was revoked. But"—Nick brightened—"he wrote and said that in another year or two he'll be able to come back. The guy he worked for is willing to sponsor him, and the problems at home have been sorted out."

"Right . . . in a year or two. Do you know how long that is?" Jake grumbled.

"I'm guessing that three hundred sixty-five days times two is not the answer you're looking for." Nick punched Jake's arm lightly. "Man, no wonder you're bummed. Short of becoming an exchange student yourself—how's your Russian?—there's nothing you can do."

"Maybe not." Jake admitted, resting his forehead in his hands and closing his eyes. Visions of Nadia instantly filled his head. He could still taste her kisses from the afternoon before in the Cave. He would never forget the pain in her eyes when they had said goodbye—and that was just an ordinary goodbye. He could barely wait to see her, to touch her again. Soon he'd have to wait forever.

No. That was not going to happen. A thought that had been drifting in the back of his mind began to take shape.

His stomach hardened into a knot. Once he took this step, there'd be no turning back. So be it. His life was about to go from being on hold to fast forward. Jake looked Nick straight in the eye. "Nadia Karloff is not going anywhere," he declared.

"Right. You're going to kidnap her and hide her from the INS. Get real, man," Nick said, putting the milk back in the refrigerator. "You don't want to start messing with those Immigration and Naturalization dudes."

Jake felt like a fool for not seeing the solution earlier. With a wide grin he stated, "I'm not going to mess with anyone from INS. I've decided Nadia's not going anywhere. She's staying right here, all nice and legal, because I'm going to marry her."

Nick stopped dead. "What?"

"You heard me. Nadia Karloff is going to be my wife." Jake paused. The look of pure shock on Nick's face made him laugh. "What's the matter, DiMartini? Aren't you going to congratulate me?"

Maybe I shouldn't have quit the paper before I got the job, Nancy thought as she parked her Mustang outside WSTN on Thursday afternoon. The two-story glass-and-concrete building sat on the edge of town near the interstate.

Nancy felt uncomfortably close to losing her nerve. She must have been crazy to think that she, a freshman, could beat out the university-wide competition to anchor the college news hour. Professor Ramirez had been encouraging, but at the Media Center library, Nancy had run into at least half a dozen other applicants she had encouraged. All were upperclassmen; most had experience; and one already produced his own public access show.

Nancy had no doubts about her ability as a crackerjack writer and reporter, but she also had no illusions about her knowledge of TV broadcasting.

Well, what are you in college for if not to learn? she asked herself. It's not like you're auditioning for CNN. Not yet.

Nancy checked herself out in the rearview mirror before heading for the building. No one was at the information desk, but a sign with an arrow pointed the way to Student Auditions. A number of signs later, Nancy found herself outside a studio door marked Student Auditions Here with an *X*.

"Nancy!" Professor Ramirez greeted her from down the hall. "Ready?" she asked, acting pleased.

"As ready as I'll ever be," Nancy replied, handing the professor the forms she had filled out.

"Unfortunately Professor Trenton has left already. I never got a chance to tell him about your audition. But he'll trust my judgment in this."

"So I won't get to meet him?" Nancy wasn't sure what that might mean.

"Not today. But if you get the job, you'll be working with him very closely. He's going to produce the first few shows, as I told you.

"Now, off to makeup. When you're done, go into the studio. The cameraman will tell you what to do. I'll be in the control booth and will meet you here afterward." The professor pointed Nancy down the hall. "Good luck!" she called out.

A few minutes later Nancy returned, feeling confident about how she looked, though still nervous. Okay, Nancy Drew, anchorwoman, go for it, she encouraged herself. The On Air warning light was off, so she knocked and walked right in.

The taping studio was small. The set, which included a couch, a coffee table, and a couple of chairs, took up half of it.

"Hi," the cameraman said. "It's just me, Frank, for the audition. Don't worry—for the show, you'll get more of a crew." Frank showed Nancy over to the sofa. "You sit here. You'll read from the text down there." He pointed to the coffee table. Concealed in its top was a TelePrompTer, with the text displayed in large letters on the screen. "But you're supposed to refer to the papers in your hand from time to time, like you're reading from them." Frank chuckled. "The trick is to try not to look like you're gazing down at all." He fixed Nancy up with a tiny earphone and microphone.

"First we check the sound level. Say something," he said. "Anything," he prompted when Nancy didn't utter a word. "Hello?" he waved at her.

"Sorry," said Nancy. "I'm a little nervous."

"Hey, don't worry. You won't get it all right, not your first time round. No one does. Just relax, do your best, and think of the camera as your friend. Now, try again."

"Good evening. I am Nancy Drew and this is *Headlines*." Nancy spoke evenly.

"Great, Nancy Drew. Now just listen to the

earphone and you'll hear which camera to look at. Just tell me when you're ready. And, remember, the camera is your friend."

After Nancy read the text of the news story through twice, she felt as ready as she'd ever be. "Okay. We might as well shoot it now," she told the man.

A voice came through the earphone, telling her to look at camera number one. It began the countdown. When the red light on camera one blinked on, Nancy began to read the news. Trying to keep one eye on the camera and one on the TelePrompTer was almost—but not quite—funny. At first Nancy's voice felt high and tense, but after several seconds, she began to get the hang of it.

When the control room cued her, she turned to face camera two, while continuing to read. Her voice was now pleasant and expressive as she reported on a local food, clothing, and book drive. She began to feel more like herself.

By the time she finished the text, Nancy felt confident she had done a good job. The red light over the camera winked out, and Nancy waited a moment before taking off her microphone and earphone.

"Good job," said Frank. "You'll give the pros a run for their money one day."

Nancy thanked Frank warmly and left the

studio. Out in the hallway, she leaned against the cinder block wall and let out a long breath.

A second later Professor Ramirez came out of the control room. "Nancy, that was just terrific. You're a natural, and the best I've auditioned. The job is yours—if you want it."

"You mean it?" Nancy grabbed the professor's hands in her excitement.

"Absolutely." Professor Ramirez laughed. "Say yes."

Nancy smiled so broadly her face hurt. "Yes!" she said loud and clear. "When can I start?"

"Whenever you want."

"Now?" Nancy gripped her briefcase.

"With that attitude, Nancy, you'll go far. The offices are right down the hall." She pointed to a large glass window at the far end of the hall. "I'll page the station manager to show you to your cubicle."

"Thank you, Professor Ramirez." Nancy could find no other words. She waited until Professor Ramirez went back into the studio, then pumped her fist in the air and softly cheered, *"Yesssss!"* Nancy headed in the direction of the offices, feeling as if she had just conquered the world.

Nancy opened the door to the glass-enclosed room and looked around. Most of the cubicles were empty.

"Nancy? Nancy Drew?" A tall young woman with brown hair walked up, her right hand outstretched. "I'm Dana Feldman, WSTN's station manager. Welcome aboard."

"Hi," Nancy answered, firmly shaking Dana's hand. "Professor Ramirez said that I could set up shop now."

"Sure thing." Dana led Nancy past cubicle after cubicle until they reached one that seemed identical to all the others. It was sparsely furnished with a desk, a file cabinet, a computer stand and computer, and two chairs. The desk was bare, except for a phone and a wire mesh in/out box. "Isabel told me you're a freshman at Wilder."

"Yes, I am. I know that's kind of unexpected," Nancy admitted.

"I don't know. I was a freshman when I got my first job at the station—as a file clerk!" Dana made a face. "Now I'm working on my thesis in communications and I'm a glorified file clerk!" Nancy laughed. She liked Dana's sense of humor.

"This is where you can hang your hat," continued Dana. "If you need anything, my extension is twenty-five. Good luck, kid!"

Nancy opened her briefcase, pulled out two new yellow legal pads, and placed them in the center of her desk. That was all she had. Later she would add her treasures: a framed photo of her dad and her old blue ceramic pencil holder, the one Bess had given her for her sixteenth birthday. It was misshapen and chipped, but it was Nancy's good luck charm and she kept it stuffed with pens. Ceremoniously she sat in her desk chair.

"I made it," she informed the walls of her cube. "Now I just have to wow Professor Trenton." Suddenly she realized her throat felt dry.

Audition nerves had made her thirsty. Before anything else, she needed to find a vending machine for a cold drink. Then she'd get to work, putting together her own news program.

CHAPTER 7

Bess threw herself across the big brass bed. She buried her face in her hands and cried her heart out, until the play's director, Jeanne Glasseburg, called out, "And, curtain!"

"Bess, that was your best job yet!" Jeanne congratulated Bess, as Bess sat up, tears still streaming down her cheeks.

A thin sound of clapping rose from the back of the Hewlitt Center theater. Bess smiled and bowed her head slightly. Brian Daglian helped her off the bed. "Great work, Bess," he said. "I'd celebrate with you, but I've got a makeup lit. exam in exactly fifteen minutes. Wish me luck," he said, tugging his sweater over his T-shirt and running a comb through his blond hair.

"Luck!" Bess said, and planted a kiss on Brian's cheek. "And thanks for all the help with this scene. By opening night we're going to be star material."

"Someone back there already thinks you are!" Brian said, waving into the dark of the auditorium. "Go," he said, giving Bess a friendly shove, "your fan is waiting."

Bess laughed as Brian left. "George, is that you?" she called, clambering down the short flight of steps leading from the stage.

"In person," George said, bowing from the waist. "You really were convincing up there. It was scary." George shivered slightly. *"Cat on a Hot Tin Roof* is a pretty intense play, and you and Brian are hot!" George hooked her arm through her cousin's. "You're a talented woman, Bess Marvin."

"And you're a good friend, George Fayne," Bess replied warmly. "You've been to more rehearsals than anyone."

"Do you mind?" George asked as Bess grabbed her coat and book bag from one of the seats.

"No, I love it. I love the support."

"Not half as much as you'll love the treat I planned," George announced, chuckling.

"Treat?" Bess's whole body stiffened. "What kind of treat?"

"Dinner out, on me, at Blake's Place. I am dying for a big, juicy burger. How about you?"

The very word *burger* set Bess's mouth watering. The thought of spending an evening just hanging out with George was tempting. But Bess couldn't risk a burger, and she knew she didn't have the willpower to settle for salad while George ordered Blake's double cheeseburger special.

"George, I'd love to, but—"

George staggered slightly. "What in the world could be more important than a Blake's burger?"

"Biology. Test coming up," Bess lied. Actually, she'd slept through so many first-period biology classes lately she had no idea when her next test was.

George sighed and tugged her stocking cap down over her thick dark hair. "Them's the breaks. But I'll give you a rain check."

"After the play is over," Bess suggested. She knew she couldn't risk any calories until she never had to wear that slip again.

"I'll take you up on that," George said.

At the bottom of the performance center steps, George headed one way across the quad to the cafeteria, while Bess started for the library. As soon as George turned the corner, Bess doubled back toward her dorm. She'd had success not eating all day so far. Now she planned to take the edge off her hunger by dipping into her new stash of candy that she just bought. She deserved it.

*   *   *

Nancy strolled back into the WSTN office, soda in hand.

"Hello, there." A male voice greeted her as she walked into the cubicle.

Nancy flinched. "Hi," she answered. A dark-haired guy wearing a maroon and white Wilder sweatshirt was at her desk. He was leaning back in the chair, his arms folded behind his head and his feet propped up on the desk. His look was one of pure arrogance. Another self-absorbed upperclassman, she thought.

She studied him frankly, her eyes following the line of his legs to the top of the desk. Her yellow pads were nowhere in sight. Maybe she was in the wrong cubicle. She glanced behind her. No, she was in the right place.

"Excuse me," she said, looking him straight in the eye. If it weren't for his self-satisfied, dimpled smirk, he could have been incredibly good-looking. "What are you doing here?" she asked, putting her soda on the desk with a decided thump. "And where's my stuff?"

"What stuff?" he asked, managing somehow to sound innocent.

Nancy began to get annoyed. "Look, I don't know who you are, but this is my desk, and I had put my stuff on it—you know, legal pads and a couple of pencils."

"Oh that . . ." He pointed to Nancy's things, neatly stacked in a corner. "I moved everything. I figured whoever left them in my office would be back later."

"*Your* office?" Nancy spoke emphatically. "I'm sorry to inform you, but this isn't *your* office. It's mine."

"No way," he said. His smile faded. He swung his legs off the desk and stood up. It had the intended effect on Nancy. He was easily six foot two, and obviously spent time working out. But the effect was broken when he opened his mouth again. "This space belongs to the anchor of *Headlines,* and that's me."

"There must be a mistake," Nancy exclaimed hotly. "This is my office, my chair, my stuff, and anchoring *Headlines* is *my* job!"

"Impossible."

"Why?" Nancy retorted. "Professor Ramirez hired me for the show less than an hour ago and gave me the go-ahead to move into *my* office."

"That's crazy." The guy was fuming. "Professor Trenton told me at my tryout earlier this afternoon that I had the position all wrapped up. He showed me my office, and I went back to campus to get my stuff."

Nancy nodded slowly and carefully adjusted the tone of her voice to sound reasonable. "I see what happened. I auditioned after you. Obviously I did a better job."

"Wrong. I was the last audition. Trenton saved the best for last. And I never even saw this Professor Ramirez."

"I never saw Professor Trenton," Nancy countered. "But Professor Ramirez hired me, and until I hear differently from her, I'm staying right here."

"All night?" The guy scoffed.

"If necessary," Nancy insisted.

"Then if we're going to spend the night together, maybe we should introduce ourselves." The hulk grinned, abruptly shifting gears. "My name's Michael Gianelli. And you are?"

He extended his hand, catching Nancy off guard. She kept her arms folded across her chest. "I'm Nancy Drew, and don't think you can con me with a smile, Michael Gianelli. I worked hard to get this job, and nothing and no one's going to get me to give it up."

That wiped the smile right off his face. "I wouldn't be so sure of that. Though you must have worked hard to get the job, because you obviously didn't win it with charm."

"Which *you* did?" Nancy scoffed, as Dana Feldman hurried into the room.

"What's going on here?" She looked at Nancy, then stared at Michael. "Who are you?" she asked him.

"Michael Gianelli," Nancy answered for him. "He says that Professor Trenton told him he was anchoring *Headlines.*"

"Just as you say that this Professor Ramirez hired you," Michael retorted.

"Time out, guys!" Dana shouted. She

looked from Nancy to Michael. "Obviously something's wrong here." She addressed Michael. "Professor Ramirez did hire Nancy. She told me so herself."

"And who are you?" Michael asked officiously.

Dana was not impressed. "For your information, I am the office manager, Dana Feldman. And Professor Ramirez asked me to show the anchor of *Headlines,* Nancy Drew, to her desk, this desk."

"You're putting me on," claimed Michael, which did nothing to raise his standing in Dana's eyes.

"No," Dana replied evenly. "But I'm sure there's been some kind of miscommunication." Half mumbling, she added, "It wouldn't be the first time." Dana reached for the phone. "Let's call the professors up and see what's going on."

"By all means," Michael said. Nancy detected a note of uncertainty in his voice. She was anticipating seeing the look on his face when he found out she was right.

Dana tried Professor Trenton first but got his answering machine. She left a message, explaining that two students were claiming to have been chosen anchor and asking him to call Professor Ramirez to settle the situation. Professor Ramirez's machine answered, too. Nancy's heart sank.

"I don't believe this," Nancy said, after Dana left the same message on the voice mail.

"I do," Dana admitted with a sigh. "I've been around Wilder's media department for years. They're great professors, but rather overextended. Mistakes happen." She turned to Nancy with an apologetic shrug. "I know Isabel promised you the job—"

"What about Professor Trenton—doesn't he count?" Michael asked sarcastically.

"Of course he does," Dana said soothingly, as if Michael were a three-year-old. "I was speaking to Nancy. Leave your numbers with me. I'll call you as soon as I hear from them. I'm sure they'll both be eager to get the whole mess settled by tomorrow morning."

Michael scribbled his phone number on a pad of paper and gave it to Dana. "I'll be waiting for your call," he stated, grabbing a worn leather bomber jacket off the back of the chair.

"As soon as I hear anything," Dana said.

Michael glared at Nancy and strode out the door, every fiber of his being radiating anger and near-mesmerizing energy.

"I'm out of here, too," Nancy said tightly. But not for long, she added to herself. She was determined that she, and not Michael Gianelli, would anchor the show.

Nancy started to pack up her things, then suddenly stopped. She looked around and saw no sign of Michael Gianelli. She turned back and carefully repositioned her legal pads on *her* desk.

CHAPTER 8

Nancy pulled into the WSTN parking lot through giant puddles of melting snow and rain at eight o'clock Friday morning. Four cars were already there: a Dodge sedan, a minivan, an old station wagon, and a bright red souped-up VW Bug. The Bug's license plate read MICHAEL.

"Is there no end to his ego?" Nancy grumbled, annoyed that Michael Gianelli had beaten her to the meeting that would settle which of them would anchor *Headlines*. The other cars must belong to Dana, Professor Ramirez, and Professor Trenton. Nancy groaned. Even though she was on time, she would appear to be late because she was the last to arrive.

She raced through the rain to the building

entrance. A minute or two later she arrived in the meeting room, dripping, and angry at the weather for giving her a bad hair day.

"Ah, Nancy." Professor Ramirez stood, both her hands outstretched. "I'm so sorry for this mix-up." Nancy took her hands. A balding, sandy-haired, slightly stocky man was standing behind Professor Ramirez.

"I'm Professor Trenton," he introduced himself. Nancy shook his hand. He had a firm, friendly grip. "And I, too, apologize for the error." He had a pleasant voice and bright eyes. He wore a bow tie with images of the Three Stooges printed on the fabric. In spite of her nerves, it made Nancy smile.

"I'm glad to meet you," she said.

Nancy took off her coat and hung it up. She shook the rain from her hair. Only then did she turn to meet Michael's gaze. He was checking her out. She wore a peach turtleneck, a brown- and black-checked blazer, and her best jeans. She knew she looked great despite her wet hair.

Michael had a resolute, hard look in his eyes. He and Nancy were both ready to fight— and draw blood, if necessary—to win.

"Hi, Nancy," Dana said as she walked in the room carrying a tray of coffee mugs and pastries. "We waited for you to start."

Nancy took the coffee but turned down the

pastries. Her stomach was on overdrive, and she was in no mood for food.

"Sorry I'm late, but the traffic was heavy," Nancy said, feeling a bit defensive. Then she regretted it. Why did she have to apologize when she knew she was on time?

There was a moment's awkward silence, broken by Professor Ramirez. "I think Sidney—Professor Trenton—and I owe both of you an apology. We got our wires crossed."

"Not for the first time," Professor Trenton said, laughing. He looked from Nancy to Michael. Neither of them returned his smile. He changed his tactic. "The short of it is that I didn't know Isabel had scheduled another audition, so I gave the job to Michael."

"I hadn't heard a word from Stanley," explained Professor Ramirez, "so I figured the job was still open. I hired Nancy."

"Then, last night, we sat down and watched both tapes together," added Professor Trenton.

"Now that I've seen Michael's tape," Professor Ramirez continued, "I see what the problem is."

Nancy's heart stopped. "What do you mean?" she asked. Michael's eyebrows arched slightly, and a smile flickered across his face.

"What she means is that you are both terrific," Professor Trenton explained. "I must say I have never seen a freshman with such poise, such confidence and maturity, in front of the camera. It's almost scary, Nancy."

Nancy colored with pride and forced herself not to gloat in front of Michael.

"Michael's had TV experience, so his performance wasn't as surprising," Professor Trenton continued. "But he has an edge—a kind of ruthless intelligence—that is exactly what the show needs." The professors exchanged glances. "So, you see, we were in a quandary. You're both perfect for the job. We have, however, come up with the perfect solution."

Isabel Ramirez broke into a big smile. "You're both hired."

"What?" Nancy and Michael exclaimed in horror.

The professors were still smiling. "Right, you'll *co*-anchor *Headlines.* Nancy, you're a very good writer, and you've got a strong, honest presence in front of the camera, which is compelling and refreshing. Michael has run Wilder's news radio program for two years now. He's got the edge on production know-how, and brings an intriguing toughness."

Professor Trenton checked his watch and got up. "So that should do it," he said, beaming. "I've got to get going now, but we'll meet first thing next week to map out plans for the show." He turned to Dana. "Call maintenance and ask them to set up *Headlines'* office in the conference room near Studio A. With two anchors we'll need more space."

He turned to Nancy and stretched out his

hand. She stared at it a moment, speechless, before giving it a halfhearted shake. As he left, she wondered if she had ever felt so disappointed and frustrated in her whole life.

"So that's it?" Nancy said weakly, speaking to no one in particular. It seemed crazy. Without warning, her hopes for running her own show had just gone up in smoke, and she was powerless to stop it. It was like some kind of bad dream.

"That's it," Professor Ramirez answered briskly, picking up her briefcase. "While I apologize for the distress this must have caused both of you, I think it's all worked out for the best." She opened the door and then turned to face Nancy and Michael. "I suggest you two get together today and start brainstorming. Call me if you need me." And she was gone.

After a few moments of silence, Michael shoved his chair aside and grabbed his backpack. His cheeks were flushed, and he looked as upset as Nancy felt.

Nancy slipped into her raincoat and pursed her lips. Well, she thought, somehow they would have to make this work. She forced herself to open her mouth. "Java Joe's this afternoon? Three o'clock?"

Michael nodded curtly and yanked the door open. "Drew and Gianelli. A real dream team," he grumbled under his breath.

"More like a nightmare!" Nancy muttered just loud enough for him to hear.

"Ah. At least we agree on that!" he countered, stalking out the door.

Nancy glanced at Dana.

"Good luck," Dana said with a small sigh. "Looks like you're going to need it."

Outside, rain was falling in sheets, washing away the patches of blackened snow. Why, oh why, does it have to rain? Stephanie moaned. Everything will be ruined, completely ruined.

She stood on her toes, craning her neck to see past the fire escape to the sidewalk below. Even as she watched, a canary yellow House and Home delivery truck pulled up.

"They're here!" she exclaimed to the empty apartment. Jonathan wasn't due home for a couple of hours.

She answered the buzzer, digging into her purse for tip money. Since she had bought everything on credit, she still had the hundred dollars in cash. A few minutes later, the deliverymen arrived, winded from the stairs.

"Mrs. Baur?" one of the men asked, as Stephanie opened the door.

"Yes," she said,

"No one told us this was a walk-up," he grumbled, wiping the sweat and rain off his face. "Where do you want the carpet?"

"In the living room," Stephanie said, showing

the way. He dropped the rolled-up carpet on the floor, while his partner tossed the plastic-wrapped pillows in a corner.

The first deliveryman took off his work gloves and pulled a delivery slip out of his jacket pocket. "Sign here, Mrs. Baur."

Stephanie had prepared herself for this moment. "Excuse me," she said, shoving all but forty dollars of the cash in the man's hand. "Would you help me arrange the furniture?" she asked, batting her eyelashes. The man checked the tip.

"By all means," he said.

When his partner returned with the lamp, Stephanie put them both to work. They rolled out the carpet, set up the lamp, and moved the battered easy chair and Jonathan's braided throw rug down to the basement.

When they left, Stephanie spent another hour cleaning the apartment and arranging the throw cushions. "There, that does it!" she exclaimed as she smoothed out the last pillow. She stepped back to survey the room.

"Perfect! Just perfect!" Stephanie pronounced, kicking off her shoes and flopping exhausted on the couch. She snuggled into the sea of cushions, feeling elegant, happy, and, for the first time since her marriage, truly at home.

"I can't wait to see the look on Jonathan's face when he walks in!" she murmured, imagining his reaction.

Slowly her smile faded. Stephanie sat up, reached for her bag, and grabbed her cigarettes. Her hand shook slightly as she lit one and took a deep drag. Jonathan was sure to love it, wasn't he?

"Jake, Jake! Are you there?" Nadia pounded on Jake's apartment door as thunder clapped outside.

"Nadia?" Jake threw open the door.

Nadia flung herself into his arms, sobbing. "Jake, it is awful. They send me away in two weeks. Just two weeks more!" She gasped for breath between words.

"Nadia!" he said, hugging her tightly. "Slow down. What's going on here? Who said you only have two weeks?"

"Immigration people." Nadia's voice shook. "Last night I talked to a lawyer in Chicago. But today I get a notice from INS. They say now the rules have changed for me. I must leave the country in two weeks."

"But they said you had over a month!" Jake suddenly felt as if the whole world were against them, against their love.

"Today I get new notice. Only two more weeks, and I will be gone. I must be gone . . . or"—her voice dropped and she shuddered—"I go to jail."

Her tears steeled Jake's resolve. "Nadia, I won't let them do that."

"You cannot stop them," she cried dramatically as Jake led her inside. He unclasped her rain-drenched cape and flung it off her shoulders. Her soft gray sweater and velvet leggings were warm and dry, though Nadia shivered. Strands of her dark hair had escaped the coquettish knot on top of her head, framing her face. Even now, she looked exquisite.

Jake drew Nadia over to the couch and lay her down, covering her with a thick quilt. He pulled off her boots and socks and rubbed the warmth back into her cold feet.

"You help me so much," Nadia said, reaching out to him. She put her hands around his neck and pulled his head down to hers. She looked deep into his eyes and then drew her lips to his. Jake seemed to melt into her.

Nadia pulled away ever so slightly. "But now it must be over," she said with fresh tears.

Jake sat up abruptly, pushing her away.

Nadia cringed. "Jake, I—I am sorry. You are angry. Life is too wretched."

"Nadia, Nadia," Jake whispered, putting a finger on her lips. "Sometimes you talk too much."

This is it, Jake thought to himself. Get on with it, before you lose your nerve.

He knelt before her on one knee.

"Nadia . . ."

"Yes, Jake," she said, perplexed.

"Will you marry me?"

CHAPTER 9

"Marry you?" Nadia repeated.

Jake saw waves of emotion wash across her face: shock, confusion, joy, and then hurt, like a small, wounded animal. Nadia leaped up off the couch. She backed toward the door, picking up her boots and cape. "You make fun of me, no?"

Jake scrambled to his feet, his heart in his throat. "No! Nadia, no, never." He reached out for her, but the room between them had opened like a chasm. "I have never been more serious in my life. You said yesterday that the only way you can stay here is to marry a U.S. citizen." Jake tugged down his frayed fisherman's sweater and made a wry face. "This is one U.S. male citizen to the rescue. Not just

101

willing, but desiring more than anything to marry one Russian female citizen, Nadia Karloff."

Nadia dropped her cape and boots to the floor and took a step toward Jake. She shook her head slowly and took a deep breath. "You do not have to do this thing. I am moved and—I think the word is *flattered.* I do not deserve such a good friend."

"Friend!" The word stung Jake.

Nadia smiled. "Oh, Jake . . . I do not mean we are just friends. I care for you so much. You must not do this just to save me. Marriage is so serious," she said, sounding wise. "And we are so young."

Jake closed his eyes, and pressed his fingers against his temples. "I know," he said, turning away from her. All his doubts and fears welled up inside again. Did he love Nadia? How would they live? Was he really ready to commit to one woman, *forever?* "Nadia, to be perfectly truthful, I wouldn't be asking you to marry me right now, if it weren't for your visa problems."

"I know," she said, sadness filling her voice as she sank back down onto the sofa.

"The point is, we need to do something, otherwise you'll be sent off to Russia within weeks. Who knows what will happen then?"

"We would stay in touch, I promise you. I would write you every day. Five times a day, at least," Nadia declared, lifting Jake's hands to her lips. She kissed each of his fingers. With each kiss, Jake's heart seemed to stop.

Jake shook his head to clear his thoughts. "Nadia, you're an extraordinary, beautiful woman. I'm sure a horde of guys in Moscow would be willing to take my place. You'd forget about me soon enough."

"Never," Nadia interrupted him sternly. "Never another guy. Never will I forget you."

"Maybe not forget, but we'd drift apart." Jake put his hand under Nadia's chin, tilting her head up. He lost himself in her eyes a moment before going on. "This visa problem may be the best thing that could happen to us. We can begin our life together a few years earlier than I planned. . . ."

Nadia put her finger on Jake's lips. "You were planning we would marry before this visa problem . . . Someday?"

Jake nodded.

"You love me that much!" Nadia's voice trembled.

"I do."

Nadia put her hands on his shoulders and knelt on the sofa facing him. "Then, Jake Collins, my answer is yes." Nadia covered Jake's face with kisses. Now her cheeks were wet with tears of joy. Jake didn't hesitate to return her kisses.

"Don't cry," he murmured. "Don't cry. Aren't you happy?"

"I have never been more happy," she sobbed, running her hands over Jake's body. "I will be your wife."

Wife. Jake tensed up at the word, then relaxed. Jake didn't believe in fear. Fear was something a guy walked up to and faced. Besides, love wasn't something to be afraid of, he told himself.

"I will not have to leave Wilder now," Nadia whispered, snuggling against his chest. "I will not have to leave you."

"Ever," Jake stated with great firmness.

"Ever," she repeated solemnly.

"Shall we tell people or keep it a secret? We could make a big surprise later, after the wedding. Are we going to elope? Like Romeo and Juliet?" Nadia asked, her eyes shining.

"Elope?" Jake sat bolt upright. "No way. I've just proposed to the greatest woman in the world, and I want the whole world to know her answer was yes. I want to shout our news from the rooftops. I want all our friends to be at our wedding."

"You think too much of me, Jake."

"No, not half enough." Jake got up and pulled Nadia to her feet. "I know the perfect time to announce our plans. Tomorrow night at Stephanie's party!"

Nadia's smile was glorious. "I forgot all

about it. My whole suite is invited. Everyone will be there!"

"Everyone," Jake said, feeling a twinge of uneasiness. Even Nancy.

"You look about as thrilled as I feel," Michael said to Nancy that afternoon at Java Joe's.

Nancy unwrapped her scarf and unbuttoned her coat as they stepped up to the counter. "At least you say what you mean," Nancy replied, trying to match Michael's tone. "All that honesty is refreshing." *When it's not rude,* she added to herself.

"Wrong," Michael stated. "You're the 're-freshing' and 'honest' one, I believe. I'm the anchor with the edge."

Nancy rankled, remembering Professor Trenton's description of her audition tape. She had been flattered to be told she had come off like such a pro at her tryout. But she hated the word *refreshing* about as much as she hated being called *spunky.*

"Two mochas, please," Michael told the waitress.

"No," said Nancy. "Make mine a double espresso." *The nerve!* Ordering for her without even asking what she wanted.

"Didn't take you as a double espresso sort of girl," Michael said, studying Nancy.

Nancy was not in the mood to be studied.

"What? Isn't espresso frothy enough for a refreshing woman like me?" she shot back.

His thick dark eyebrows arched up. Nancy was beginning to recognize the movement as a Michael Gianelli trademark. *"Frothy* would be the last word I'd choose to describe you."

His quickness surprised Nancy. Their coffees showed up, and before Michael had a chance to take out his money, Nancy plunked down her two dollars on the counter, picked up her espresso, and made her way to the far corner table. If Michael Gianelli thought he was calling all the shots, she'd show him otherwise.

She watched Michael make his way through the tightly packed tables of the crowded shop. Broad-shouldered and tall, he looked simply too big for Java Joe's. It was petty, but she couldn't help enjoying the sight of him being jostled a bit by the afternoon coffee crowd. As he squeezed into the small space opposite her at the table, Nancy braced herself for more inane commentary from Mr. Ego. But Michael surprised her.

Setting his cup down, he launched right into the heart of the matter. "So how are we going to make this work—being co-anchors?" He smoothed back his thick black hair and Nancy noticed that he wore an earring. "Neither of us wants to be in this situation, but unless you quit . . ." He let his words hang in the air.

Nancy smiled wryly. "I've never quite gotten the knack of writing a resignation letter."

Michael met her gaze. "Didn't think so."

"Let's clear the air about one thing," Nancy stated. "We've been hired as *co*-anchors. That means neither one of us—"

"Is in charge?" Michael suggested, with the shadow of a smile.

"Unfortunately," Nancy said, hating the way he had interrupted to finish her sentence for her. "Since we have no choice, let's try to work together."

"Or at least not against each other," Michael added, leaning toward Nancy.

She leaned back away from him. His intensity set her nerves on edge. He made her want to keep her distance. Hold on, she said to herself. That's just what he wants—for me to back off. "Maybe," she suggested, leaning forward again, "we should try to find common ground."

"That's easy—*Headlines* is our common ground. I want hard-hitting, up-to-the-minute news stories of interest to the Wilder community."

"Problem is, we're a once-a-week show, Michael. Hot news items happen daily. Concentrating on breaking news just won't work with a weekly format."

Michael gave a condescending smile. "Really, Nancy," he said. "This is TV we're talking about, not some newspaper. We can tape a news segment moments before we go on air."

Nancy wanted to kick herself. "Of course," she admitted ruefully. "I'm used to the lead time we need on the paper."

"Bogged down in that old print media mentality," Michael diagnosed, in a patronizing tone that made Nancy want to scream. "So, as I see it, we run with the latest hottest story, be it foreign, domestic, or local, and tie it in with life at Wilder. Get the man-about-campus point of view."

"How about student-about-campus . . . women go to Wilder, too," Nancy reprimanded him.

"Whatever turns you on," replied Michael.

Nancy took a deep breath and tried to stay calm. "Just because TV allows us to run with a breaking story, that doesn't mean heavy news is the best use of our airtime. You can watch the evening news for that. *Headlines* is a weekly college show. We need hard-hitting features that have a direct impact on Wilder students. For instance, how changes in federal scholarship policy affect individual lives on campus. We can have panel discussions, call-ins, on-line hook-ups across campus—"

"Now that's novel!" Michael's voice dripped with sarcasm. "Sounds positively Oprah Winfrey. Good woman's stuff, scarcely academically challenging."

"Woman's stuff!" Nancy cried. Calm was now out of the question.

"Yeah," he sailed on. "Just what I expected. Now it's obvious why the profs wanted a man on board."

Nancy fought to keep her temper. "They chose us both because we're good, hard-nosed reporters, each of whom has something different to offer." Nancy threw up her hands. "So, let's at least try to *listen* to each other."

"Maybe you should take your own advice and listen to me instead of finishing my sentences."

"Finishing *your* sentences? What do you think—"

"—I've been doing?" Michael finished, swirling his cup and studying the dregs of his coffee. "I can't help it if I have a quick mind."

And a big mouth, Nancy commented silently, and immediately regretted not having said it out loud. She folded her hands demurely in front of her and smiled. "This doesn't seem very productive to me," she said.

Michael eyed her warily. Good, I've got him on guard, Nancy thought. "No, I guess it doesn't," he admitted slowly.

"So what do we do about it?"

He shrugged. "I intend to present my ideas to Professor Trenton first thing Monday. I'm sure he'll agree with my hard-edged approach. That's what they hired me for."

"No," Nancy retorted. "Edginess. Professor Ramirez was simply impressed with your edginess—"

"Edge—"

"There you go again," Nancy countered swiftly. "Interrupting."

Now Michael threw up his hands. He started to say something, then mimed zipping his mouth shut.

Nancy dug into her backpack and presented Michael with a file folder. "Here's my proposal. Hard-hitting, human interest features. I've made a list of possibilities and mapped out three complete shows. I faxed copies to both the professors before we met."

"Before we met?" Michael bellowed. "We were supposed to talk first."

Nancy downed the rest of her espresso. "As I figured it, it wouldn't matter much, one way or another." She paused and checked her watch. "After twenty minutes, nothing you've said has changed my mind about the direction of the show. And nothing I've said has—"

"—made a dent," Michael declared, a set expression on his face.

Nancy had to fight back a compelling urge to stick her tongue out at him.

"I'm sorry to break up this stimulating discussion," he announced, pushing back his chair. "But it seems I have some faxing to do. Professor Trenton will just have to choose."

"But he told us to work it out between us. It's our job to plan the show's format," Nancy reminded him.

"Maybe so. But a small problem's cropped up."

"Like what?" Nancy said through her teeth.

"You—you're impossible to work with!"

Nancy fumed as she watched him shoulder his way back to the door. Before he got outside, however, Nancy found her tongue. "At least my ego fits through the front door!" she yelled. Every head in the café turned, except Michael's. He didn't break his stride as he slammed the door behind him. She watched him through the window, shaking her head in disgust.

Pausing outside Java Joe's, Michael turned up the collar of his jacket and then bent his head into the wind. His step was strong and purposeful. He was definitely going to be a formidable opponent. He had a quick tongue, and Nancy had to admit that he was one of the smartest guys she'd ever met. Why, of all the men at Wilder, did she have to end up working with him?

Nancy thought again that most girls would find him incredibly attractive. Until, of course, he opened his mouth and came out with some biting, arrogant comment.

*   *   *

"Men!" Leslie King declared, slamming her door with a loud bang.

Her roommate's sudden entrance caught Bess in the middle of one of her binges. She instantly stuffed the tail end of a Twinkie in her mouth, washed it down with diet soda, and kicked her shoe box of treats under her desk. "What are you doing here?" she asked, as soon as she could get her breath.

"Football!" Leslie snorted, tossing her camel hair coat on the bed. "Nathan stood me up for the NFL. Not just the NFL, but some rerun of some old game. Nathan Kress is sitting in front of a TV in the lounge with a bunch of his buddies, being a sports junkie. This is supposed to happen to my mother. To my aunt. To old people. Not to me."

After a few minutes of Leslie's nonstop ranting, Bess sighed and tuned her out. She had counted on Leslie not being in their room for the evening.

She had hoped to have some privacy because she couldn't bear to eat in public anymore. She felt sure everyone in the cafeteria was looking at her and thinking she should be dieting, not dining.

Bess was starving. In fact, lately she was always starving. All she could think about, day and night, was food. Unless, of course, she was onstage.

Onstage, she entered another world, a place

where her stomach didn't cry out and her mind didn't hallucinate hamburgers.

Bess glanced at Leslie out of the corner of her eye. Leslie was pulling off her boots, and still going on about Nathan. Keeping one eye on Leslie, Bess reached for the shoe box under her desk and tried to pick it up and slip it into her bottom desk drawer.

"Bess?" Leslie's voice made Bess jump. The contents of the box spilled out on the floor. Great move, Marvin! Bess got down and shoved all the candy, cupcakes, chips, and empty wrappers back inside. "What are you doing?" Leslie asked.

"Nothing," Bess said, slamming the cover on the box and shoving it under her bed, where she usually kept it hidden. She stood up and faced her roommate. The sudden movement of standing made Bess's stomach lurch, and she felt dizzy.

Leslie's green eyes narrowed. "Bess, you look sick again."

Bess took a giant step toward the door, but had to stop to hold on to her desk chair to keep from falling. The room had started to spin. "I *am* sick. I'd better go to the bathroom." Leslie moved in quickly and blocked her way.

"Bess, we have to talk."

"Not now, Leslie."

"Now." Leslie insisted. "I have a very good idea what's going on here."

"What, do you have an instant medical degree or something?" Bess tried to laugh.

"No. But I've been observing you for a while, and you've got a problem."

"Nothing new about that," Bess said offhandedly. "Things haven't been great lately, but they are looking up. You said so yourself recently."

"Yes. I did," Leslie admitted grudgingly. "But they also seem to have taken a weird turn—I think you're developing an eating problem."

Bess's knees went weak. "Come off it, Leslie. I've never had a problem eating. You of all people know eating's my passion."

"Wrong. Lately I haven't seen you eat one real meal. But here in the room you've been bingeing on junk and then running off to the bathroom. Bingeing and purging, Bess."

Bess felt herself break out in a cold sweat. "That's crazy. You're crazy."

Leslie stood firm. "I am not. I know what I'm talking about. I've read up on this. It's a disease. The symptoms are eating in secret and, afterward, throwing up so you don't put on weight. It's called bulimia. It can kill you."

Bess clapped her hands over her ears. She glared at Leslie. "Shut up. Shut up, now! The brainy Leslie King tries to prove she's an expert on everything. This time you've gone too far," Bess screamed. She grabbed her jacket and strode past Leslie and out of the room.

Bess decided against using the bathroom on their floor. Leslie might follow her in there. Instead, she took the stairs down to the lobby and made a beeline for the bathroom there. Thank goodness. The place was empty.

A few minutes later Bess came out of the stall and washed her face at the sink. She looked up at her reflection in the mirror. Dark circles had formed beneath her eyes. Her complexion looked positively green.

Good job, Bess, she moaned. She slid her back down the wall and sat on the floor, hunched into a tight little ball. Suddenly, wrenching sobs came from deep within her. She sat there and cried until she could cry no more.

CHAPTER 10

When Nancy returned to her dorm after dinner that evening, she found Suite 301 empty. She went into her room and checked her answering machine. There was one message.

"Nancy," began a man's voice she didn't recognize. "Sidney Trenton here."

Nancy grinned and continued to listen. "Got your fax. Very enterprising. I love your ideas for features."

"All right!" Nancy cheered.

"Your human interest stories will dovetail nicely with Michael's take on how to divide the show between breaking news and soft-sell fillers. Glad your meeting was productive. See you next week at our planning session. Good work!"

Dovetail nicely with Michael's take on how to divide the show? Filler items? Was Gianelli for real? "Who does he think he is!" Nancy cried, exasperated. He had actually conned the professor into thinking they had collaborated on the format for *Headlines*. Of all the nerve!

Nancy caught sight of her face in the mirror. She looked so frustrated, she had to laugh. Get off it, Drew. You're the one who mentioned faxing Trenton to begin with. If you hadn't been so intent on one-upping him, Michael wouldn't have dreamed of faxing Trenton.

Her machine beeped and launched into the second message.

"Hi, Nancy."

Michael? She hadn't given him her number. Of course, he must have gotten it from the student directory. Nancy stared skeptically at the machine, as Michael's voice continued. He was so sure she'd recognize him, he didn't even introduce himself. That figured.

"Productive meeting. Good thinking, faxing Trenton. Took you up on it. He phoned me already, and we discussed my proposal."

"His proposal. Right!" Nancy tapped her foot impatiently, her hands on her hips.

"Thought we could brainstorm some more on the phone, but you're not there. Makes sense that a girl like you wouldn't be holed up in a dorm on Friday night. By the way, Trenton said he liked those fluffy fillers you suggested—or was the word *frothy?* Michael's mockery hung in the air until the machine clicked off.

"You are absolutely obnoxious, Michael Gianelli," Nancy yelled to the empty suite. Then, kicking off her shoes, she had to chuckle. The guy seemed to know exactly how to push all her buttons. Well, she didn't have to like him, she just had to work with him. With that, Nancy grabbed a notepad and headed for the common room. She flicked on CNN, sat on the floor with a soda by her side, and propped a notebook on her knees.

She was lost in her work when the door of the suite burst open. She looked up to see Jake stagger in, carrying Nadia across the threshold.

They were both laughing hysterically. "I don't think I've got the hang of this," Jake gasped, putting Nadia down. Nadia kept her arm around Jake's neck, while planting a big kiss on his lips.

"Hi, guys!" Nancy greeted them, feeling pretty awkward.

Jake's and Nadia's lips came unglued.

"Nancy, uh—hi!" Jake said.

"I thought everyone was at Club Z," Nadia said, her arms still draped around Jake's neck. As she talked, she absently curled her fingers through Jake's hair.

"Everyone but me," Nancy pointed out. She was obviously intruding on some sort of very private moment. But she had every right to be in the lounge. They were intruding on her. Besides, they were more than likely headed for Nadia's room. Nancy leaned back on her elbows and smiled.

Nadia and Jake turned back toward each other, oblivious to Nancy's presence.

"What's up with you guys anyway?" Nancy interrupted their reverie. "You look so . . . so . . ."

"Ecstatic?" Jake finished. "Should we tell her?" he asked Nadia in a loud whisper.

Nadia's hands flew to his mouth. "Jake, no! It is our secret." She dissolved in giggles.

Jake grinned at Nancy. "I'll give you a hint." He circled Nadia's waist with his arms. "Nadia's troubles are over!"

"Troubles?" For a moment Nancy had no idea what Jake was talking about. Then she remembered. "With your visa?"

"No more trouble. Now I stay," Nadia said. "But that is not the best part. Right, Jake?"

"Right!" he declared.

"How?" Nancy marveled.

Nadia and Jake exchanged adoring glances. Jake propped his chin on Nadia's head and smiled from ear to ear. "We're getting married!"

Nancy was stunned.

"Now, Nancy, please tell no one," Nadia begged, clasping her hands in front of her.

"Not until tomorrow night. We're announcing it at Stephanie's party," Jake said.

Nancy managed to nod.

"So mum's the word?" Jake put his finger to his lips.

Nancy finally found her voice. "Uh—of course."

The voice in Nancy's head, however, spoke more to the point. How did Nadia manage this?

Stephanie stood at the kitchen table, wrapped in an apron, feeling bewildered. " 'Use sour cream, yogurt, or cottage cheese as the base for your dip,' " she read from the cookbook propped open in front of her. "But which, you idiot!" she yelled, jabbing the book with the wire whisk she was holding. The book fell on the floor, knocking over the measuring cup full of chopped chives on its way.

"This is not the life of Stephanie Keats! It can't be!" she cried in frustration as she cleaned up the mess.

Of course it isn't. It's the married life of Stephanie Baur. Stephanie pursed her lips. She had wanted to get married, and if learning to cook was part of being married, she was determined to do it.

Stephanie's face lit up when she finally heard Jonathan's key turn in the lock. "Jonathan!" she cried, rushing to the door. "House and

Home delivered everything." She flung open the door, grabbed his hands, and put them over his eyes. "Don't peek!"

"Whoa!" Jonathan protested with a laugh. "What's going on here?"

"You'll see!" Stephanie guided him into the living room, reached out, and flicked on the light. "Tah-dah!" she sang with a flourish. "You can look now! Don't you love it?"

He opened his eyes and the smile instantly died on his lips. "What's all this stuff?"

"Don't you like it?" she asked, even though she knew exactly what he was thinking.

"Like it?" Jonathan shook his head. "What's 'like' got to do with it, Stephanie? How much did all this cost?"

Stephanie swallowed hard. "Look, I know what we agreed on, but I just couldn't bear to buy junk. Besides, that's bad economy. Everything here is high quality and will last for years—"

"Or until you decide you prefer a pink carpet to this weird brown!" Jonathan cried, angrily. "How in the world did you pay for it? Don't tell me you used the credit card."

"The payments won't be that much, forty dollars—or a little more—a month and—"

"We'll be celebrating our fifteenth anniversary before this is paid off." Jonathan moaned. "It all goes back tomorrow morning."

"No, Jonathan!" she cried, her cheeks burning.

"We had an agreement: a tight budget until you finished school and got a real job. The stuff goes back, period."

"No way. Our party is tomorrow night. I refuse to have people see our place looking like a disgusting hovel!"

"Hovel?" Jonathan repeated. He took a deep breath. "Look, the party was your idea. You want it? Fine, you give it. But our friends will just have to take us the way we are. This stuff gets moved out of here first thing tomorrow."

"Next you're going to say we should move the old stuff back in."

"Right. Where is it?"

"In the basement, en route to the garbage, where it belongs," she snapped.

"I'll get the superintendent to move it up before the party," he promised.

"Well, you'd better call House and Home, too, because I won't!" Stephanie cried, tears welling up in her eyes. With a scathing glance, she marched past him, and into the bedroom, slamming the door so hard the walls shook.

The campus clock had just struck 1:00 A.M. when Nancy decided to turn in.

Her suitemates were still out partying at Club Z. Jake had left a while ago. Nancy padded down the short hall toward the bathroom. As she passed Nadia's room, she heard her speaking in Russian in a low, urgent tone. Nancy slowed her pace and listened.

Nadia was making another mysterious call to Russia, Nancy thought, but then realized that Nadia had probably called home to tell her parents her big news. That would be normal enough, except why would her voice be so low and sound so secretive?

Nancy clutched her terry robe and continued down the hall. Jake Collins getting married. It made no sense. But then nothing about Nadia and Jake made sense. It had all happened too fast. The Jake that Nancy knew would never, ever rush into marriage. He had big plans for his life, ambitions to travel the world as a correspondent, to work for a major news organization. Marrying young sure didn't fit in with his dreams. It was, Nancy reflected, as if Nadia had cast a spell over him.

And what about that photograph covered with hearts? Nancy couldn't shake the impression that it was a wedding picture—from Nadia's own wedding.

Nancy had one hand on the bathroom door when Nadia's laughter rang out. She spoke quickly in what sounded like a mocking tone, and then Nancy caught Jake's name. Nadia lowered her volume quickly and spoke in a sultry, coaxing voice. There was another brief silence, broken once again by Nadia's low, sexy laugh. No one ever laughed with their parents like that. Next Nancy heard what sounded like kissing noises and then the receiver clicked down.

Nancy wished she knew some Russian. She sighed and leaned back against the wall. However much she'd like to stay out of Jake's life, she couldn't stand by and watch him marry Nadia—especially if Nadia was already married to her so-called brother. Nancy bet that was the person she had been speaking to on the phone.

Nadia was quite possibly using Jake, marrying him to get a green card to stay in the United States. And he thought it was love!

Nancy knew she had to solve this puzzle, but, oh, how she wished that just once a mystery would solve itself.

CHAPTER 11

So, what do you think Leslie wants?" George asked Nancy as they sat down at the Bumblebee Diner. The off-campus hangout was bustling with the Saturday morning breakfast crowd. "She made a big thing of meeting us where we wouldn't run into Bess."

Nancy laughed. "True enough. Once Bess found out she had to wear nothing but a slip onstage, it was Diet City. Bumblebee's pancake special is definitely not part of anyone's healthy diet plan."

George laughed along with Nancy. "My take is that Leslie has some scheme up her sleeve that she doesn't want Bess to know about. Like a surprise party for opening night."

Nancy's eyes did not light up at the thought.

"From the sound of Leslie's message, I think Bess may be in trouble. I just hope you're right and I'm wrong. In any case, we're about to find out. Here comes Leslie."

Watching Leslie wind her way through the crowd to their booth, George groaned. "Why do I get the feeling that you're right and I'm wrong?" she asked under her breath.

"Hi, you two," Leslie said tonelessly. She hung her coat on one of the hooks at the end of the booth and sat down. "Thanks for coming out so early to meet me."

Leslie was carrying a plastic bag with a shoe box inside. Where can you shop for shoes at this hour? Nancy wondered. Leslie deposited the shopping bag on the seat beside her. Her hand remained on top of it.

"Doesn't take much to lure me to the Bumblebee Saturday mornings," George quipped.

"What's up, Leslie?" Nancy asked.

The waitress appeared with coffee, and the three placed their orders before Leslie answered Nancy's question. "Bess has a problem."

Nancy nodded as she exchanged a glance with George.

"It's serious," Leslie stated. "I think she's bulimic."

"Get out of here!" George scoffed.

"Bess?" Nancy asked. "She's been dieting

because of the play, but bulimia? What makes you say that?"

Leslie unfolded her napkin and folded it up again. "She's bingeing and purging. It's been going on for a while now. I'm scared she's going to get really sick if she doesn't get help."

Nancy eyed Leslie carefully. "I don't know, Leslie. Bess likes food too much."

"Come to think of it," said George, growing thoughtful, "I haven't seen her eat a thing for ages. Every time I ask her to come to dinner or lunch she has an excuse."

"But not eating is anorexia," Nancy interjected.

"You're right, but not eating in public is one of the symptoms of bulimia," Leslie explained. She smiled ruefully. "I've been looking into it, and she has all the signs. She doesn't want people to see her eat. Once she's alone she stuffs herself with junk food. Then she goes off to the bathroom and throws up. It's classic. I caught her the other night."

Nancy shuddered. "That's got to make a mess of your body."

"How can you get any nutrients if you don't digest your food?" George's voice shook slightly. "She could wind up killing herself."

"Hold on, George," Leslie said. "I don't think she's there yet."

"But why is she doing this?" Nancy wondered aloud. "It can't just be the costume."

"I don't think it's the costume at all," Leslie said. "It's still all about Paul."

George hit herself on the side of her head. "Of course. We keep thinking she's over Paul's death. Like getting over the flu or something. Man, she loved that guy, and he's dead. It's going to take a long time to heal."

"She probably feels out of control," Leslie suggested. "Bulimia, like other eating problems, has to do with trying to be in total control of your life. Only it all backfires."

Leslie paused. Clearing her throat, she said, "Here's the evidence." She picked up the shopping bag from beside her on the seat, and pulled out the shoe box. She set it in front of Nancy and George. "Open it."

The shoe box was stuffed with empty candy wrappers, half-eaten bags of chips and pretzels, and almost every other type of junk food.

"Bess keeps this under her bed. For nights now she's been up, munching on this stuff. I pretend I'm sleeping. After she eats, she gets up and goes to the bathroom, and . . ." Leslie bit her lip.

The three girls fell silent. Finally Nancy spoke up. "We have to do something about this."

"How?" George asked. She started to pour sugar into her coffee but suddenly stopped. The sugar content of the junk in Bess's shoe box made her think twice.

"I tried to talk to her. She wouldn't listen to me," Leslie said. "But you guys might be able to get through to her."

"Sounds like she needs professional help," Nancy ventured.

"I guess it's up to us to convince her of that," George said.

"Someone has to," Leslie explained. "You're the best ones to do it because you're her closest friends. She needs your support."

"Don't worry," Nancy said. "George and I will get on her case. And we won't let up until she gets counseling. She has rehearsal today. We'll corner her afterward."

The cast of *Cat on a Hot Tin Roof* spilled out of the Hewlitt Theater Saturday afternoon, weary from a long rehearsal.

"See ya later!" Bess called back over her shoulder as she headed down the steps. With rehearsal over, Bess began to think about food and how to stay away from it. That seemed to be all she thought about recently. Her stomach felt odd and her head ached. She longed to go back to her room and sleep. Except her room was off-limits—at least until she could face Leslie again without wanting to kill her.

"Bess! Wait up!" George called.

Bess smiled and looked over her shoulder. Her smile froze. George was with Nancy. Nancy wore a familiar, determined expression.

Oh, great! Bess groaned inwardly. Leslie must have talked about last night.

George hooked her arm through Bess's as they caught up to her. "We've got to talk."

"Now?" Bess stopped and disengaged her arm from George's. "But I've got to—"

"Now!" Nancy and George declared in unison.

A few minutes later Bess found herself in George's room, perched on the edge of one of the beds.

Bess decided to get this over with as soon as possible. "Okay, guys, what's going on here? You both look like someone has died or something." Bess laughed tightly. "Whoops, I'm not supposed to say things like that."

"Bess, you can say whatever you want," Nancy began, "but Leslie believes you've got a problem."

"Oh, that. She's on one of her amateur shrink kicks. She'll get over it." Bess grinned first at Nancy, then at George. They didn't smile back. "Hey, you two, stop looking like the grim twins. Because I've had a funny stomach lately, Leslie started jumping to conclusions. Believe me, I'm fine. Just fine. Don't I look it?"

"No," George replied bluntly. "Your color resembles leftover canned peas."

"Ugh." Bess gripped her stomach clownishly. "Don't make me sick."

"You're the one making yourself sick," Nancy said. Bess's heart stopped. "George and I went to the library and found this book on eating disorders."

"The only eating disorder I have is loving food too much." Bess tried to laugh but only managed a smile.

"Listen," George said, opening the book. " 'Bulimia: an eating disorder characterized by cycles of bingeing, purging, and dieting.' " George closed the health science textbook. "Sound familiar?"

Bess stared at her hands. "Not really," she said, fighting to steady her voice.

Nancy took Bess's shoe box out of her backpack.

"Where'd you get that?" Bess cried, horrified to see Nancy holding her private stash.

"Bess," Nancy said gently, "Leslie gave this to us this morning."

Bess just stared. She felt betrayed and exposed.

"Bess?" Nancy touched her arm. It was as if she had pressed some kind of button. Bess felt empty. Then the tears began to flood the emptiness inside her. "Oh . . ." She wept. "I'm so ashamed. I-I'm sorry. I'm so . . ." Bess's tears choked off her words.

George sat down next to Bess on the bed and began rubbing her shoulders. "Bess, hey, it'll be okay. You don't need to feel ashamed or sorry."

"We love you, Bess," Nancy said as she knelt beside Bess on the bed and took her hand. "That's why we had to confront you with this."

Bess sagged against Nancy as her tears slowly began to subside. "I don't know what went wrong," she murmured. "I thought everything would be okay if I could get my eating under control. I was so afraid I'd look fat in that costume. And now *everything* feels so wrong. I'm scared," she confessed, bursting into a new round of tears.

"Bess, this isn't the end of the world," Nancy said softly.

Bess looked up at Nancy and read hope in her eyes. "You could have fooled me," she tried to joke.

"It's just a problem, one there's plenty of help for," George said so matter-of-factly that Bess's tears dried right up. "We're here for you, and there are others, too."

"We'll help you every step of the way." Nancy reached in her bag and drew out a handful of pamphlets. "I got these at the library. There's a help line listed for counseling for eating disorders."

Bess took the pamphlets and turned them over. " 'All calls confidential,' " she read out loud. "That's good, because I have never felt so embarrassed in all my life," she admitted in a small voice.

"Bess, if you want, we'll eat every single meal with you until you get over this," Nancy pledged.

"We can go with you to Student Services to make an appointment with a counselor. But Bess," George cautioned, "you have to help yourself after that."

Bess sat silently a moment. She felt frightened and scared and . . . "You know what," she said, looking into Nancy's eyes, "I feel relieved. I feel like a little kid who's been doing something sneaky, and I've been found out, and I'm really, really glad."

On the way back from Jamison Hall, Nancy stopped at Java Joe's. She felt overwhelmed with Bess's troubles, Nadia's suspect behavior, and her own battle with Mr. Egomaniac Gianelli.

Over a double decaf cappuccino, Nancy thought about not being in control. Half the time at college she felt out of control. Pressures—academic, social, and financial—seemed to bombard her and other students endlessly. What to do?

First, Nancy told herself, take a deep breath. Then sort through the problems one by one. Decide what you can exert control over and what you have to let go of. Michael Gianelli was not someone she could control, she decided. Their problems were going to take a long time to solve. Nancy had left Bess in good hands with George, and Bess's problems, too, now fell into the category of things needing a long-term solution. That left Nadia.

Nancy now knew exactly where she had to start—with Nadia. Julie Akimoto, Nancy's friend from her literature class, worked in the foreign exchange program office. She would have as much information as anyone about Nadia and her deportation.

Without looking, Nancy jumped up and started for the phone in Java Joe's. As she whirled around, she charged right into someone, coffee flew everywhere.

"Oh," Nancy cried. "I'm so sorry!"

"Don't mention it."

Nancy focused on her victim. "Julie? Julie Akimoto?" Nancy burst out laughing.

"Nancy, I was coming over to say hi. I didn't expect such an enthusiastic reception."

"I was just getting up to call you. I need to talk to you." Nancy and Julie sat down. "Can I get you another coffee?" Nancy asked.

"It's not necessary," Julie said. "I can't stay long. I can get one to go on my way out."

"Do you know the name Nadia Karloff?" Nancy began.

"Funny you should mention her—another coincidence," Julie said. "I just filed her papers this morning. She's the Russian girl whose father is a poet, right?"

"Right. Then you must know about her getting deported."

Julie shook her head. "Whoever told you that must have got it wrong. Nadia Karloff's papers are in order. Like I said, I filed them just a couple of hours ago. Believe me, I would have noticed."

"You're sure?"

"Positive. No way she's getting deported. Though—I shouldn't be telling you this—she sure had trouble coming to Wilder in the first place."

"Why?"

Julie smiled wryly. "The usual problem: money. She had trouble proving she could survive in the States for the duration of her education without having to hold a job."

"That's really weird," Nancy mused aloud. Money problems didn't fit with a shopping spree.

"Anyway, Nadia's visa is just fine," Julie continued. "At least until she graduates. Then she'll have to go back to Russia—unless she finds some other way to get a green card or start the citizenship process."

Nancy shook her head slowly. She'd heard all she needed. Marrying Jake was one way to stay in the country. But what was the big rush?

"Julie, I have one more question."

"Shoot, Nancy."

"Did you happen to notice Nadia's marital status?"

"Sorry, but no. I have no idea, but I assume she's single."

Nancy looked serious. "Julie, could you check it out for me? This is really important."

"Why?" Julie asked. "I'm not supposed to do that sort of thing. I could get in big trouble."

"Please, Julie," Nancy pleaded. "I'll tell you my suspicions, if you promise not to mention them to anyone. Then you'll see why I need you to do this."

"Nancy, you're starting to sound like James Bond!"

"I think Nadia may already have a husband in Russia. And now she's secretly going to marry Jake Collins so she can stay in the U.S. But please, don't tell anyone about this. Who knows what will happen if Nadia finds out I'm checking up on her?"

"Don't tell me any more. I have the feeling the less I know, the better. I'll check and call you later."

CHAPTER 12

On her way back to Thayer Hall, Nancy tried to figure out what Nadia was up to, from her point of view. She's married to a man in Russia. She loves him, judging from the romantic tone of her phone calls. She wants to stay in the United States and can do that only by marrying a U.S. citizen. She gets Jake to marry her. Then what? Nancy gave up. There were still too many blanks to be filled in. Not to mention the mystery of the designer jeans.

Nancy made up her mind to corner Nadia before she left for Stephanie's party. Part of Nancy wished she could mind her own business. But this was serious business. Nadia Karloff was a fraud.

The door to Casey and Nadia's room was

ajar. Nancy knocked anyway. "Nadia?" She pushed on the door and it swung open.

Nadia glanced up from her desk, startled. She slid the letter she had been reading into her desk drawer.

"Nancy," she said. "I am not dressed yet. It gets late, no?"

"This won't take long," Nancy said.

Reaching for her dress, Nadia slipped it carefully over her head. It was long, and the foggy gray material shimmered. "You like my dress?" she asked, spinning in front of the mirror, holding the slim skirt out a little.

"Love it," Nancy admitted, not in the mood for small talk.

"Nancy, I am sorry I do not know you well, yet. But you have been very nice to me. This relationship between me and Jake must not be—how do you say—comfortable for you. You are a very big-spirited person."

"Thank you, but, Nadia, let's cut the small talk," Nancy said. "I'm not in the mood for games right now."

"What kind of games?" Nadia countered, picking up her hairbrush.

"Visa games?" Nancy suggested, with a tight smile.

"Immigration does not play games," Nadia said, addressing Nancy's reflection.

"No, but you do. What's really going on with your visa?"

Nadia stopped brushing her hair. "This is not your business, Nancy. Stay out of it."

"Not on your life," Nancy retorted, and sat at the foot of Nadia's bed.

Nadia narrowed her eyes at Nancy. "Please. Stop your questions. You will cause a lot of problems—for everyone."

"I think you are the one causing problems for everyone," Nancy pointed out coolly. "You've been lying about being deported. You're conning Jake into marrying you. He has a right to know what's going on."

"What are you talking about?"

At the sound of Jake's voice, Nancy whirled around. "Jake!" He was standing in the doorway.

"Oh, Jake!" Nadia flew across the room and into his arms. As he pressed her head to his chest, he glared over her shoulder at Nancy, furious.

"What's going on here, Nancy?" he asked, his expression grim.

Nancy felt frustrated. She wanted to tell him everything, but would he listen to her? She doubted it.

"Ask Nadia," she said, slipping past him.

With one hand on the doorknob, she looked back over her shoulder at Nadia. "You'd better tell him the truth before tonight, or I will." Then she closed the door softly and walked down the hall.

* * *

"What's with her?" Jake asked after Nancy closed the door.

Nadia burst into tears. She clutched Jake's shirt and sobbed into his chest. "Oh, Jake. She is so jealous. She makes believe she does not care that we love each other, Jake, but she will do anything to stop us—" Nadia broke off, racked with tears.

"Don't cry, Nadia, don't cry like that," Jake said. He rubbed her back. How could Nancy hurt Nadia like this? And tonight of all nights.

"Nancy's just jealous," Jake repeated as Nadia's sobs began to subside. Boy, Nancy sure had him fooled. All along she had insisted she wanted to be his friend. Now Jake felt betrayed, angry, and strangely disappointed.

"She has no right to do this to you, Nadia."

Nadia pushed her hands against Jake's chest and stepped back. "Nancy is going to ruin everything."

"Oh, Nadia," Jake declared passionately. "She can't." He smiled at Nadia. "If Immigration can't come between us, Nancy can't." He searched Nadia's eyes, and the smile died on his lips. "Nadia? What did Nancy say?"

"Nancy has been nosing around my records here at Wilder."

"What? Why?" Had Nancy lost it, or what? Jake wondered. "What's this got to do with our wedding?" Jake searched his mind. Did Nancy have some kind of plan to sabotage the wedding, or maybe the party tonight? Part of him refused to believe he could be so wrong about a woman he had once loved. But until five minutes ago he would have bet a million bucks that Nancy didn't have a jealous bone in her body.

"Maybe she wants trouble between us . . . so I do not marry you."

"Nancy can nose around all she wants. She can't stop me from marrying you," Jake insisted.

Nadia hung her head. "Jake, Nancy cannot. But she was right about one thing. Maybe the truth will." She folded her arms across her chest. "The lies have to stop. Now."

"Lies?" Jake hoped he'd heard wrong.

"Jake, do not make this harder. I have to tell you something. Everything must come out in the open. Everything," she cried passionately, her lips trembling.

"You've been lying to me?" he made himself ask.

Nadia flinched. She turned away from him, and hung her head. "Yes. I have, Jake. My name is not Nadia Karloff, it is Elena. Elena Markova. I come to States under false passport. It is forged. I needed to leave Russia, quickly. My life, the life of my whole family is in danger there."

"What?" Jake felt as if the floor had turned

141

to quicksand. He reached over, making Nadia face him. "You're putting me on."

"Why would I do that?" Nadia asked, pushing him aside. She went to the window and looked out. "When I come to Wilder I think I am safe. At least until graduation. By then, maybe my problems at home would die down. Or my father will take care of everything."

"Your father, the poet?" Jake asked, with a tight laugh.

"He is not a poet," Nadia said flatly. "Just like I am not who I say I am."

Jake felt duped. "So you fed me this line, and I fell for it. Like an idiot."

"Jake, this is not your fault. I did not know when I came here that I would fall in love like this." Nadia threw up her hands. "Do you think I want this to happen? I should never have had that interview in the paper. If they never see my name and photograph, they would not have suspected anything."

"They? So, we're back to Immigration. You think they found you in the *Wilder Times?* Nadia, I doubt they have a subscription."

Nadia started to speak. Jake put up his hand. "I don't need to hear more," he said, starting for the door.

Nadia barred his way. "Please, Jake," she begged, her eyes swimming with tears. "Please listen. Let me explain."

Jake shook his head, but couldn't take his

eyes off her. The pain in her face was so real. He felt a faint surge of hope. "Okay. I'll listen."

"Thank you," she said. "I cannot tell you everything, because it is dangerous to know too much. My father is a businessman. He is in trouble with a gang in Russia. I do not know English word, but they want money to protect him from other gangs. He will not pay. We are now all in danger."

"The Russian mob?"

"Please," she begged in a whisper. "Do not talk so openly of that. You have no idea . . ."

Actually, Jake did. He had read about criminal elements in Russia and how some of the recent immigrants to the States were connected to crime syndicates back home.

"So, say I believe you, Nadia. What's this have to do with you and me?"

Nadia shivered. "Nothing. Nothing really, except—" She seemed to fish for the right word. "I was warned unofficially that Immigration had, how do you say it, wised up to me. I will be deported soon. That is the truth."

"Who warned you?"

"Jake, I cannot answer that. But I have friends here. Russian friends who watch out for me." Nadia paused, studying Jake's face. "Oh, you do not believe me, do you?" she cried.

Jake slowly shook his head. "Nadia, maybe I'm nuts. But I do. I really do believe you."

Nadia's whole being seemed to lighten up. "Oh, Jake, I do not care what happens to me now. As long as I know you trust me. Whatever else I have lied about," she said, her voice trembling, "the truth is, I love you."

Jake walked up to her slowly and brushed her hair off her face. "Me, too," he said finally. "Truth is, I love you."

He drew her into his arms.

Nadia slipped out of his grasp. "No, Jake. It is too easy just to kiss and say nothing has changed. When Immigration sends me back to Russia I will know, no matter what, our love was real."

"Back to Russia?" Jake didn't follow.

"What else can I do?"

"Marry me! Aren't you the woman I asked to be my wife?"

"But, Jake, you will still marry me, after everything?"

"You bet I will," Jake answered. "Nothing's really changed. I wish you could have trusted me with all of this before. . . ."

Nadia shook her head vehemently. "No. I could not. For myself alone, yes. But for my family, I could not risk this. But now Nancy . . ."

"Nancy knows all this?" Jake had forgotten all about Nancy.

"No. I do not think so. She only knows that Wilder University knows nothing of my visa problems."

"That's good. Nancy is not exactly a person you want to have investigating your legal status here."

"Why?" Nadia asked, a note of fear in her voice.

"Let's just say she's a born investigative reporter—at least as good as yours truly," Jake admitted wryly. "But forget about Nancy. Pretty soon she won't be able to cause us any more trouble."

"What do you mean?"

"Nadia, I know we talked of getting married next Saturday, but let's move it all up. We got our license today. We'll go to City Hall, Tuesday first thing, and get married, if we can. If not we'll do it the first possible day we're legally allowed to."

Nadia put her hand to her mouth. "You are serious? You really will marry me? And sooner than before?"

"Yes." Jake was sure of that.

Nadia threw her arms around Jake's neck. "How do I deserve a man like you? I lie, and you forgive me."

Jake gently held her away at arm's length.

"Please?" he begged her now. "Don't lie again."

"Never. I swear." And Nadia sealed her promise with a long, slow kiss.

Nancy stood in front of her mirror. Her hair was swept up into a thick French twist, secured with a sparkly hair ornament. In her slim black pants and black camisole top she looked like a pretty hot party animal. But she didn't feel like one.

The last thing Nancy felt like doing was partying at Stephanie's housewarming.

Nancy had hoped that Julie would call before Nadia and Jake left for the party, but not ten minutes ago, Nancy had overheard the two of them leaving Nadia's room. They had been talking softly and laughing together. The engagement was obviously still on.

The phone finally rang as Nancy finished putting on her lipstick.

She answered the phone. "Julie?"

"Yep. I'm going to make this short. It makes me awfully nervous. Nadia's passport says that she's single, but her Wilder application says she's married. I guess no one ever thought to compare them. We always use the passport as the definitive I.D. I can't tell you which is right. Sorry."

"Julie, you're wonderful. Thank you. I owe you one." Nancy hung up. She still didn't know whether Nadia was married, but the fact that the forms didn't agree was enough for Nancy to cause Nadia big trouble.

Nancy grabbed her bag and headed out the door. She stopped outside of Nadia and Casey's room. "Casey?" Nancy called through the door.

No one answered. Nancy hesitated, then walked right in.

She went straight to Nadia's desk and quickly looked through the papers on top of the desk. Nothing struck her as extraordinary. Overdue library book notices. Notes for a term paper. A couple of letters in business envelopes. Stuff about working as a foreign exchange camp counselor. No clue there as to what game Nadia was playing.

Nancy tried the drawers. Inside the top drawer was a sheaf of letters tied together with a big purple ribbon. "This is more like it!" Nancy murmured. She carefully removed the top envelope. It was addressed to Nadia, in English. The return address was in Russian, but Nancy noted that the postal stamp was from Moscow. Both addresses were written in a bold strong hand, with black ink. She turned the envelope over.

"Ah-hah!" she exclaimed. The envelope was covered with lots of little hearts drawn in red ink just like the hearts on Nadia's love note to Jake.

Nancy pulled out the letter. She couldn't

read a word of it. What had she expected? A translation?

Right! Nancy brightened. A translation. One of Stephanie's best friends was a Russian language major. She was bound to be at the party. Pocketing the letter, Nancy left the room. In a few hours she hoped to have all the pieces to Nadia's puzzle.

"You do forgive me?" Stephanie asked Jonathan. It was almost eight o'clock. Their party was about to start, but Stephanie needed to know, now, that she hadn't blown it with Jonathan.

Jonathan stopped combing his hair, and turned to her. He straightened the spaghetti strap of her short black dress. His touch on her bare shoulder was incredibly tender. It didn't send a thrill down her spine, but it made her feel loved.

"Stephanie, couples fight. It's normal. It's okay. We both got a little crazy last night about the furniture." He pulled her in front of him and made them both face the mirror. "We love each other. Besides," he said, his eyes gleaming wickedly, "how can I stay mad at such a beautiful woman?"

Stephanie laughed a low, throaty laugh. "So, when I'm old and ugly, you'll stay mad?"

"We'll be too rich by then to fight over

money," he said, nuzzling her head with his chin.

Jonathan hooked his fingers under the thin straps of her dress. "Too bad guests are coming. . . ." he said sadly.

Stephanie slipped away from him. "Jonathan, let's be serious."

"What, don't I look serious?" he teased.

He did. But Stephanie realized even if no one was coming, she wasn't in the mood for cuddling just then.

"I mean it. I want you to know that I went overboard with the furniture. I shouldn't have bought all that stuff. You were right all along."

"You mean you think we can survive on thrift-shop-trendy?"

"Trendy?" Stephanie arched her eyebrows. "I wouldn't go that far. But I promise from now on I won't get carried away when I shop. I've learned my lesson."

"And I've learned mine," Jonathan said, surprising her. "I was rigid, and I went a little wild."

"Hmmm, I like wild!" Stephanie said, as they headed into the living room. The braided rug was back. The lamp was gone. But at least Jonathan had let her keep the cushions.

Jonathan pulled her down next to him on the couch.

"Jonathan, people will be here in ten minutes," she said, getting right up and heading for the kitchen.

"Ten whole minutes . . ." he murmured, following her. He came up behind her and buried his face in her hair.

"Jonathan . . . my hair . . ." she began to protest. Then the doorbell rang.

"Saved by the bell," she said, sliding away from him.

"I hate early birds," Jonathan grumbled, pulling away from her and straightening his shirt.

"Me, too," Stephanie said, wondering why she felt so relieved.

When Nancy, Bess, and George arrived at Stephanie's apartment, the party was in full swing. Music blared. The small living room was packed. People were dancing in the kitchen, and even more were crowded into the tiny bedroom. Nancy caught a glimpse of Jake and Nadia. They were leaning against the window, completely absorbed with each other. No question, the engagement's on, Nancy thought ruefully.

"Happy housewarming!" the three cried in unison as Stephanie came to greet them.

"I think everyone is here," said Stephanie, obviously pleased with the turnout. "In case anyone wants to know, Will's over in the corner, talking to Casey and Ginny."

"That's my cue. See you guys later." George wiggled her way through the crowd and greeted Will with a big hug.

A moment later Bess spotted Brian and took off. Alone with Stephanie, Nancy asked, "Steph, what's your friend's name, the one who studies Russian?"

"Shana. Shana Stein," Stephanie answered, swaying her hips to the beat of the music.

Nancy raised her voice over the noise. "She here?"

"Yes. In the kitchen. She's making some kind of dessert."

Nancy thanked Stephanie and made her way to the kitchen. Couples were dancing in a corner by the stove. Shana was at the table, cutting open a pineapple. She was short and plump, with frizzy red hair and freckles. "Shana?"

Shana looked up and smiled broadly. "Nancy. Great party, no?"

"Terrific," Nancy said, grabbing some chips. "You speak Russian?"

"Da!" Shana said. "Some, at least—though Professor Grigori might disagree. Why?"

This was no place for Nancy to bring out Nadia's letter. "Look, can I talk to you out in the hall? I can barely hear myself think in here!"

"Sure," Shana said, wiping her hands. She followed Nancy out of the apartment.

Nancy motioned Shana to the end of the narrow hallway, and sat down at the foot of the stairs leading up to the roof. Someone had propped the door open, and the cool air was refreshing. "I know this seems a little weird," Nancy charged ahead, "but I need someone to translate this letter."

"A pen pal?" Shana asked, taking the letter from Nancy's hand.

"No, it's not my letter," Nancy said bluntly. "If you feel uncomfortable with this . . . but, Shana, it is very, very important."

Shana's eyes gleamed. "Hey, reading other people's mail is everyone's secret passion, isn't it?" She took the envelope, and her eyebrows shot up. "This is addressed to Nadia Karloff."

Nancy nodded. She knew when it was better not to try to explain.

Shana shrugged and opened the letter. "It's from someone named Leo." She scanned the page. "That's funny. It says 'Dear Elena.' "

Nancy drew back, shocked. "Elena? Who's Elena?"

"Probably Nadia . . . maybe Nadia's her nickname." Shana began to read to herself. "I can't get every word but the gist of it is that this guy named Leo is arriving in the U.S.— the day after tomorrow, Monday, in Chicago. Then he connects with a plane that lands here in Weston at three o'clock in the afternoon. He says he can't wait to see her again and that he can't believe how well their plan is working out." Shana looked up, blushing a little. "Maybe I'm misreading the rest, but I think it gets . . . well, sort of personal. It sounds like they're . . . well, he's more than a friend. Here, he signs it 'Your loving first husband.'" Shana looked bleakly at Nancy. "Nadia's been married before!"

Nancy nodded. "Shana," she said urgently. "Don't mention a word of this to anyone. No matter what happens tonight. Please?"

Shana's eyes widened. "No . . . of course not. I mean, reading someone else's mail may be everyone's secret passion, but it's supposed to be kept secret. Still—Jake should . . ."

"Don't worry about Jake. I'll explain everything to him."

Nancy pocketed the letter. Here was proof. Nadia—or Elena, or whatever name she was using—was some kind of con artist and Jake was the dupe. First, get married; then, get citizenship; ditch whoever she had conned into marrying her; then run off with this Leo guy— her husband.

The wedding had to be stopped.

Jake chose his moment carefully. He had wanted Nancy to be nearby when he made his big announcement. He wanted to see her face.

"Hey, gang!" he shouted over the din. "A toast to Stephanie and Jonathan."

Voices picked up the cry. "A toast! A toast!" People jostled one another to refill their glasses.

Jake grabbed a drink and put one arm around Nadia. "Here's to the Baurs, who have proved that married life can be fun. Three cheers for Stephanie and Jonathan!"

He led everyone in a rowdy cheer. Out of the corner of his eye, he saw Nadia glancing nervously at Nancy, who was standing by the door. Nancy looked like a volcano about to erupt. Jake bent over and nuzzled Nadia's ear. "Hey, she can't stop us. No one can now!" he murmured.

Jake shouted again for attention.

"If this is married life, I say, let's all go for it!" Everyone laughed and cheered. Jake grinned. "In fact, Nadia and I have decided to follow their example. I wanted you all to be the first to know. We're tying the knot Tuesday at City Hall. Everyone's invited to Club Z Tuesday night to celebrate with us."

Instead of roars of good wishes, the room buzzed with gasps and whispers. Nadia sagged slightly against him. "What?" Jake jeered loudly. "No congratulations?"

It took a second, then everyone began cheering and talking at once. "You're serious!" Casey blurted out. She turned to Nadia. "This is wonderful . . . Just such a surprise. It happened so fast."

"Yes, it is fast," Nadia said, lowering her gaze. A moment later she raised her head in triumph. "But, in Russia, we say, 'When happiness comes, do not let it fly away.'"

"Way to go, Jake!" Will pounded him on the shoulder. "You're a braver man than I am." He turned and hugged Nadia.

"You're a lucky man, Jake!" Jonathan called out.

"Lucky Nadia!" responded Stephanie.

"Yes." Nadia spoke up quickly. "Lucky Nadia. Jake is the best friend I could ever have."

Well-wishers mobbed them, and Jake soon found himself across the room from Nadia, shaking hands. He felt terrific.

"Jake, we have to talk."

Nancy's voice rattled Jake.

"I'm not sure I'm still talking to you—now or ever."

"Then I'll do the talking. You listen." Nancy's eyes were steely. "We can go outside, or talk here," she said in a low, firm voice. "It's up to you. I don't care who hears." She paused. "But you might."

"If you ruin this night for Nadia, I'll never forgive you."

"I'll risk that," Nancy said. Her tone was impossibly even.

Jake caved in. "Okay. Outside, then. Make it quick."

They went into the hall, and Nancy closed the apartment door behind them. She leaned against it. "Nadia does not love you, Jake."

Jake had prepared himself for just such nonsense. "That's a low blow, Nancy."

"There's more," she said very quietly. "I wish I didn't have to be the person to tell you this—"

"Yeah, you and me both," snapped Jake.

"Her name isn't Nadia—"

Jake broke in again. "It's Elena. Elena Markova." The expression on Nancy's face was worth this whole ordeal.

Nancy gasped. "You know?"

"Yes. Nadia told me all about it before the party, Nancy. And that's all you need to know."

"You're going to marry someone who actually lied to you about her own name?"

"Yes. Not that it's any of your business. Nadia told me everything."

"Everything?" Nancy scoffed. "Even about her husband back in Russia?"

"Oh, Nancy! You expect me to believe that?" Jake burst out laughing.

Nancy closed her eyes and took a deep breath. "Jake, I'm not saying this to hurt you. If you don't believe me, ask her. Ask Nadia about Leo. He's back in Russia right now, or"—she checked her watch—"actually he's on his way here. He's flying in from Moscow. He's meeting Elena, or Nadia, Monday afternoon at the Weston airport. He's taking the three o'clock flight in from O'Hare."

Jake's stomach clenched. He felt as if he'd just swallowed a truckload of concrete. No, this couldn't be true. But could Nancy, *would* Nancy, make all that up? He breathed deeply to calm himself.

Then comprehension dawned. "You almost got me there. . . ." He began to laugh. The release felt wonderful.

"I'm not joking," Nancy said, putting her hand on his arm.

He pulled away from her. "No. You're not joking. At first I couldn't figure it out, but it's obvious. You're jealous. You'll stoop to anything to stop our relationship." Jake took a step toward the door.

Nancy stepped away. "Jake, you must believe me when I say I'm not jealous. I'm trying to help you save your life."

"Sure. Like I'm supposed to believe that. Gimme a break." He opened the door, then looked over his shoulder. "Funny, I used to respect an investigative reporter who looks a lot like you."

CHAPTER 13

On Monday afternoon Stephanie stepped on the escalator at House and Home, squared her shoulders, and prepared to swallow her pride.

Not that she had much pride left. She felt as if it had been shipped back to the store along with her rug and lamp. The salesman had called her that morning and told her she needed to come into the store to sign the return receipt. As if she didn't feel embarrassed enough, without facing him again. Better to get it over with.

Except for the salesman, the furniture department was deserted. The man was sitting at the desk, his blond head bent over some paperwork.

"Hello?" Stephanie said, peeling off her gloves.

He looked up. At the sight of her, he smiled. "Mrs. Baur, I'm so sorry to make you come in like this. But store policy says whoever signed the credit slip has to sign the return receipt."

"I understand," Stephanie said. He handed her some papers and a pen. His fingers brushed hers. A bolt of warmth shot up her arm, startling her. She glanced up quickly. He caught her eye, before looking away. What a flirt!

After signing the papers, Stephanie shoved them across the table. She didn't feel much like flirting back. She wanted to get the whole humiliating scene over with and never walk back in this store again. "That should do it," Stephanie said shakily. She rose with as much dignity as she could muster and began to put on her gloves.

"Um, may I ask you something?" the salesman inquired, following her toward the escalator.

Stephanie turned around. "Sure."

"Why did you return the rug and lamp? You seemed so happy with your choices the other day. Was the rug the wrong color once you got it home?" He sounded so kind.

Stephanie met his understanding eyes. "No. Not at all. In fact," she told him, "it was perfect. Just perfect."

"But why then?"

Stephanie lost her self-control and told the truth. "I spent too much. My husband said we couldn't afford it." She added quickly, "He was right. We can't. The problem is I never thought I'd have to live this way. I grew up with such nice things." Her voice broke. Stephanie swallowed hard. She would not allow herself to cry. Not in public. Not in front of a cute stranger. "I've got to go," she mumbled as a sob worked its way up her throat. She broke down.

"Oh, please, Mrs. Baur . . ."

"Stephanie," she blubbered. She hated being called "Mrs." It made her feel old and dull, and as drab as Jonathan's couch.

"Here." The salesman pulled out a handkerchief. "It's clean," he said, offering it to her. He took her elbow. Stephanie let him steer her off the main sales floor, into one of the alcoves set up like a model living room.

She sank down into the plush sofa and blew her nose. "Now that was pretty dumb," she said, feeling like a wimp.

"Crying's not dumb," he said soothingly, sitting next to her. "It seems to me that what you need right now is a shoulder to cry on. A friend."

Stephanie's head snapped up. Well, he did have big shoulders. She laughed weakly. "I don't even know your name," she said, folding his handkerchief and handing it back to him.

"Kyle. Kyle Dalquist, at your service," he said, his blue eyes sparkling.

Nancy sat in her room at her computer, one eye on the screen, the other on her watch.

If Shana's reading of Nadia's letter was right, Nadia should be leaving for the airport any minute to meet Leo's plane. How Jake would deal with the truth, when it finally surfaced, Nancy had no idea. She even wondered if she should just stop caring and let the chips fall where they may. But she couldn't. Jake was a friend.

Sure enough, as the watch hands pointed to two o'clock, Nancy heard Nadia's door open, then quietly click shut. Nadia's boot heels clicked down the hall, across the lounge, and out the door. Nancy picked up the phone and dialed Jake's number.

The phone rang twice before Jake picked up.

"Jake, it's me—Nancy," she said.

"Just the person I was hoping to hear from," he said sarcastically.

Nancy flinched. "I know you won't want to hear this. . . ."

"Then why bother calling me?"

"Jake, Nadia's just left. According to my information Nadia is supposed to be meeting her husband from Russia in an hour. I'm going to drive out to the airport." Nancy took a breath. "I want you to come with me. To see for yourself what she's up to."

"That's sick," Jake exclaimed hotly. "You were out of line last night, but now you've gone way too far. Nadia isn't married—not yet—and you know it. You just can't stand the fact that I'll be her husband and not yours. If you can't face that fact, that's your problem, Nancy. Not mine, not Nadia's. Now get off our case." He slammed down the phone.

"Jake!" Nancy cried into the receiver. She punched Redial on her phone. The line was busy. Nancy hung up, forced herself to count to ten, then dialed again. Busy.

Jake had taken the phone off the hook. Now what? If she wanted to catch Nadia meeting the flight from O'Hare, she had to leave now. But if she went alone, no matter what she saw, Jake would never believe her.

Nancy had to have a witness. He trusted George and Bess, she thought, even though they were *her* friends. She called George and arranged to meet her and Bess in front of Jamison Hall in a few minutes. She'd explain what was happening on the way to the airport. As an afterthought, Nancy asked George to bring her Polaroid camera. She wanted proof to offer Jake if her hunch about Nadia and Leo proved right.

And if I'm wrong? Nancy thought. I'll feel

like the world's biggest fool. But, hey, she'd made major league goof-ups before.

Nancy was halfway out the door when the phone rang. She grabbed the receiver before the second ring. "Jake?" she cried.

"Nancy, it's me. Julie Akimoto."

"Julie? Is something wrong? I can't really talk now. I'm in a rush."

"Wait. It's about Nadia Karloff."

Nancy caught her breath. "What about Nadia?"

"I'm here in the Admissions office. Someone from the INS phoned my boss this morning and requested access to a student's records. Guess whose?"

"Nadia's," Nancy answered grimly.

"Right. Except her name's not even Nadia."

"I know, Julie. I found that out last night. She's Elena something or other."

"Markova," Julie informed her. "But this is the scary part. The Immigration guy says she might be part of a smuggling ring."

"Smuggling?" For a split second Nancy was stunned. Duping Jake to wrangle a green card and citizenship was bad enough. Two-timing him made it even worse. But smuggling? Smuggling was big-time criminal stuff. "Smuggling what?"

"Kids in Russia are hot on American clothing, particularly designer labels. They cost a fortune in the stores. But on the black market, he said, they're cheaper. He said something about CDs and software, too," Julie answered.

That was it! Nadia's spending spree at Berrigan's, her jeans by the dozen, were to be smuggled into Russia and sold on the black market.

"Anyway, the guy just left, but he gave me his number in case I heard anything about her. He might come and check out the dorm. I thought you should know."

"He won't find Nadia here," Nancy said.

All at once Nancy knew exactly what to do to help Jake. To stop Nadia.

"Julie," Nancy said. "Call that INS man back right away. Tell him Nadia's on her way to the Weston airport to pick up a man flying in from Russia. I have a feeling the man is Nadia's husband and that the agent will want to ask both of them some questions."

"If I were married to a girl as beautiful as you, I'd buy her the world," Kyle told Stephanie as they sat next to each other on the couch in House and Home's model living room.

Stephanie's eyebrows shot up. Kyle looked sheepish. "Okay, not the world. Would you settle for a designer sofa?"

"That's a new sales pitch!" Stephanie chuckled.

Kyle clutched his hand over his heart. "You wound me!" He gazed at Stephanie. "Hey, friend," he said, touching her arm lightly, "at least I got you laughing again."

"So you did," she said, wondering at what point she had stopped crying and started smiling.

He took her hand. His touch made Stephanie suddenly feel very cared for. Her dreary apartment, her saggy couch, seemed a universe away.

"You know I might have been kidding about the furniture, but a beautiful woman like you . . . I can't help feeling Jonathan doesn't appreciate what he's got."

Now that Kyle mentioned it, Stephanie realized, she hadn't felt appreciated very much at all lately. Jonathan seemed to have pampered her more when they were dating.

"Hey, don't look so sad."

"I'm not sad," Stephanie said with a proud toss of her head. Suddenly he leaned a little closer. Stephanie knew she should leave. She knew exactly what was about to happen. She adored this moment, the suspense just before a first kiss. She looked from his eyes, to the strong, straight line of his nose, to his square, firm jaw. She found herself staring at his lips, they were full and sexy, and a moment later, they were touching hers.

Closing her eyes, Stephanie put her hands on his face. Without another thought, she began kissing him back. His kisses were strong and sweet.

He pressed her to him, and suddenly his touch made her eyes fly open. "No!" she gasped, and jumped up. She stared into his blue eyes. His blond curls looked a little mussed. He had the sweetest smile. But it was the wrong smile, the wrong eyes. Kyle Dalquist was nothing compared to her dear Jonathan.

"Kyle," she said breathlessly. "I'm sorry. I— I don't know what came over me." She bit her lower lip, turned on her heel and ran down the escalator.

Stephanie felt like the worst, most awful person in the world. What kind of wife was she? She had married Jonathan so she'd stop cheating on him. Now she had betrayed him.

Head down, Stephanie raced out of the store, and just grazed a baby stroller.

"Oh!" the mother and Stephanie exclaimed in unison.

"I'm so sorry," Stephanie cried, dropping to her knees in front of the baby. He was sound asleep. One fist was in his mouth, the other curled on his blue plaid blanket. Stephanie's heart did a flip-flop, and she fell in love on the spot. "Is he okay?"

"He's fine. I wasn't looking. . . ."

"I wasn't looking either," Stephanie said. She watched as the woman continued pushing the stroller down the block. The woman wasn't much older than Stephanie. Stephanie smiled.

As she walked away, a thought slowly took root in Stephanie's mind: a baby. That's what was missing. Something to cement their bond. A baby to love. A baby for Jonathan.

CHAPTER 14

The brakes of Nancy's Mustang squealed as she turned off the ramp of the interstate and headed toward the Weston airport. She was pushing the speed limit, but according to the dashboard clock, Leo's plane had already landed.

"I hope we're not too late," she declared, exasperated. "I can't believe I let myself get so low on gas." After picking up George and Bess at Jamison, Nancy had had to find a service station. When she finally did there were three cars in front of her.

"This whole thing with Nadia feels so unreal," Bess remarked from the backseat. Nancy had filled her two friends in on the whole story while they waited for gas. "I barely know

Nadia—or Elena—but she seemed so nice at the party. And I'd kill to look like her. The whole thing with her and Jake seemed so romantic!" Bess hesitated. "Hope you don't mind my saying that."

"Why would I mind? She swept him off his feet. Even if Nadia were on the up-and-up, she was moving too fast. Jake isn't ready to marry anyone. Most of us aren't."

George nodded. "That's for sure. Though I can see how Jake fell for her. I didn't get to know her well, but I talked with her at your suite, Nancy. She had me fooled—I thought she was great. I told everyone Casey stumbled on a real treasure after Stephanie had moved out. So I guess if that INS man is right, Jake's not the only person who's been duped."

"Don't I know it," Nancy said as they pulled into the lot. "I hope Immigration catches up with her, but I don't want Jake to get hurt."

"Oh, he's going to hurt—however this turns out," Bess commented wisely as Nancy parked near the terminal.

Nancy jumped out of the car and raced for the door. George was right behind her. Bess brought up the rear. "Where's your camera?" Nancy asked George, as they hurried through the terminal door.

"Right here," George answered, pulling it out of her backpack.

Nancy didn't bother to check the arrivals

board. She simply scanned the passengers on their way to the baggage claim area. As she hurried along, she kept an eye out for Nadia. The tall beauty should stand out. "What if we missed her?" she cried.

Bess suddenly grabbed Nancy's arm and pointed to the gate. Nancy saw Nadia. She appeared to be worried as she studied the thinning crowd of deplaning passengers.

Then, all at once, Nadia's face broke into a sunny smile. She took a few steps forward. A handsome man with high cheekbones and light brown hair hurried up to her.

"What a hunk!" Bess remarked as Nadia threw herself into his arms.

Nancy watched angrily as Nadia covered the man's face with kisses. "That's the man in Nadia's photo. That's Leo," she finally said.

George whistled under her breath.

"George, your camera," Nancy ordered. "I want proof for Jake. She might make up a story that this guy's her brother or cousin or something. It wouldn't be the first time."

"Some way to greet a brother," George said, handing Nancy the camera. "Maybe that's the way you greet your brother in Russia."

"George," chided Nancy. "That's *not* funny. That is *not* her brother. He's her husband."

Nancy moved cautiously, staying in the thick of the crowd to shield herself from Nadia and Leo. Not that they'd notice anything the way they were making out. Nancy crept as close as she dared, aimed the Polaroid, and shot her pictures, one after another, without pause.

The flashes were blinding.

Nadia and Leo jumped. Nadia whirled around. "You!" she cried, pushing Leo behind her. "What are you doing here?"

"Gathering evidence. Jake won't believe what I tell him, but he'll more than likely believe what he can see." Nancy raised the camera in the air.

"You wouldn't dare!" Nadia cried, turning frantically to Leo. He started for Nancy's camera.

Nancy swiftly handed it off to George, who stood poised to run if Leo decided to pursue the matter. "Oh, but I have dared, Nadia. I've got plenty of shots that will interest Jake." Nancy paused momentarily. "Oh," she said casually, "and the INS agent who is on his way here will probably like duplicate prints."

"INS agent? Immigration?" Nadia paled.

"Yes, Nadia—or would you prefer Elena?" Nancy asked pointedly. "We all know that using Jake was just part of your plan. Leo, your husband here—we haven't been introduced, Leo; I'm Nancy Drew—and your phony name have more to do with your real scam. The INS knows about your smuggling."

Nancy would never forget the look of pure panic on Nadia's face. Leo said something to

Nadia in Russian. Nancy couldn't understand him, but his tone was urgent.

He grabbed Nadia's arm and started pulling her away.

Nadia resisted a moment. She looked at Nancy, her doelike eyes filled with pure hatred. "I hope you're satisfied, Nancy. You are a no-good, nosy idiot. I hate you. And do not think Jake will love you for this either. He will hate you, too. He is not so bright maybe, but a very good person," Nadia shouted, as she ran hand in hand with Leo.

Jake drove his car right up to the entrance of the passenger terminal of the Weston airport. He parked next to a sign that said No Standing Anytime.

Nancy had said Nadia would be meeting a three o'clock flight. It was twenty after three now. Jake jumped out of his car and rushed into the building, his keys still in his hand.

A small part of him still believed—or hoped—Nancy was wrong. Even if Nadia was meeting someone at the airport, there could be a perfectly natural explanation. Maybe her brother had flown in from Moscow for the wedding. Maybe her father had managed to slip out of the country. Jake ran his hands through his already mussed hair. But why wouldn't Nadia have told him herself?

Because Nancy had to be right. She had a

way of finding out the truth about people. But another guy, a husband? Nadia could fake a name, even a passport, but no one could fake the love he saw in her eyes. If there was a husband, maybe she was trying to get away from him. . . .

But Jake's reporter's sense told him that Nadia was hiding something. She had said that she would be in her room studying all day. After hanging up on Nancy earlier, he had picked up the phone and called Nadia. All he got was an answering machine.

Inside the airport, Jake hurried straight toward the information desk to check the arrivals board. The flight from O'Hare had landed on time.

He started for the gate. A flash of shiny dark hair caught his eye. The woman was wrapped in a familiar black cape. "Nadia," he started to call out, but then realized that she wasn't alone. She was hurrying across the terminal, hand in hand with a man. She stopped, turned back toward the gate, and started yelling at someone. Jake followed the direction of Nadia's tirade and saw Nancy.

Suddenly Nadia and her friend broke into a full run, heading in Jake's direction, toward the side exit, where there was a taxi stand.

Jake ducked behind a post. Suddenly he felt less like a player in the game and more like an investigative reporter, observing from the sidelines. He had to see how this would play out—no matter what Nadia did, no matter what happened. For one last time he tried to come up with a plausible explanation for all this. The guy's coloring was not at all like Nadia's, but he had the same Slavic cheekbones and exotic looks. Be her brother, Jake prayed.

When the couple ducked out the door, Jake took a few steps in their direction. Through the glass window he saw Nadia stop, wind her arms around her "brother," and give him a long, passionate kiss before hopping into a taxi. Jake could practically taste their kiss. He stood paralyzed, not able to breathe. He felt as though someone had just kicked him in the gut.

"Nancy, there's Jake!" George cried, gripping Nancy's arm and pointing with her other hand, the one that held the camera.

Beyond the baggage carousel, Nancy saw Jake standing dumbstruck, staring at the door that Nadia and Leo had just raced through.

"So he turned up after all." Nancy expected to feel justified, but instead she felt only deep sadness.

Before she started toward Jake, she asked George to check on Nadia and Leo, even though she assumed they had gotten away in a cab. Nancy wondered what in the world she could say to take the hurt off Jake's face. Before she got to him a commotion at the ticket counter caught her attention.

Bess gasped. "Is that the guy from the INS?" Bess pointed to a man displaying a badge to the sales agents.

"Good guess," Nancy said as George returned and told her Nadia was gone. "We'd better let the agent know Nadia's left the terminal." She reached the man in time to hear him questioning a flight attendant.

"Can you check your passenger list? A man called Leo Markov should have been on that plane."

Markov! Nancy gasped. It had to be true. Elena and Leo Markov were husband and wife.

"Excuse me," Nancy said, stepping up to the man. She glimpsed the name on his badge. "Agent Pool?" she asked. "Are you from the INS?"

The INS agent regarded Nancy warily. "Yes."

Nancy explained that she was Nadia's suitemate at Wilder and told the man what had just happened. "She just left the airport in a taxi with that guy Leo." She handed the man the Polaroid snapshots.

Looking at the photos, the INS agent cursed under his breath. "Sorry for the language, miss," he said. "It's just that it's them all right. And I missed them." Agent Pool shook his head. "If she's who I think she is, she's part of a very savvy smuggling ring. We think part of the scam involves her becoming a citizen in order to elude our network. But we'll catch up with her, and him, sooner or later." He thanked Nancy and gave her his card. Nancy promised to call if she heard from Nadia or learned anything new about her. The agent headed outside to see if he could spot the couple, but they were long gone.

"Did that guy say something about smuggling?" Jake asked, sounding shell-shocked. He had slowly made his way over to Nancy, Bess, and George.

"You heard that. . . ." Nancy said, almost afraid to look directly at Jake.

"I heard everything," he said dully. Then he put his hand on Nancy's shoulder and led her a little distance away from George and Bess. "I wouldn't be surprised if you never spoke to me again, after what I said last night and today. I just want to say . . . I can't think of anything more to say than I'm sorry . . . and thanks."

Nancy squeezed his hand.

"Where do you think they went?" Jake asked. The plaintive note in his voice cut Nancy to the quick.

"We don't know, Jake," Nancy answered tenderly. Then she frowned, her face flushed. "Where is my brain today? Nadia had no idea we'd come after her here. She probably wasn't planning on leaving town or anything."

"Not until after the wedding," Jake reminded himself bitterly.

"Even if she had to split suddenly, she'd never leave behind all her booty," Bess said.

"The dorm!" cried Nancy, Bess, and George together.

Half an hour later they stood in front of Nadia's room. The door was open. The place had been ransacked.

"She beat us to it," Nancy said, annoyed. Nadia was going to get away with everything. The thought of that made Nancy sick.

Nancy walked into the room, George and Bess following. Jake hung back by the door, leaning against the frame. Nancy had never seen him so depressed. "She was in one big rush," Nancy murmured.

Casey's bed was made, her dresser was neat. Nadia's side was a mess. Papers littered the floor, schoolbooks and notepads were scattered everywhere. The closets were empty, her shopping bags gone.

"Nan, look at this," George exclaimed suddenly. She was sitting on the edge of Nadia's desk, holding an envelope.

"She left a note," Jake cried, his voice full of hope. He crossed the room in two steps.

George bit her lip. "Jake, it's for Nancy," she said.

Nancy's eyes met Jake's. She opened the note and read it once to herself, then out loud.

"Nancy Drew:
Are you finally satisfied? You have a mean spirit and a nasty mind. Too bad you could not keep your thoughts to yourself. But maybe all is for the best now. Leo and I will not be apart. Somehow I will stay in this country. I will become a citizen—Leo, too. I know how to get what I want. If America is full of suckers like I find at Wilder, I should do very well here. Yes?"

The room was silent. Nancy glanced at Jake, whose eyes were focused on his feet.

"There's a P.S. for you," she said, and handed him the note.

Jake took a deep breath. His face turned ashen as he read. "I guess there's nothing personal about this," he said tightly. "Not anymore." In a low voice, he read.

"Jake—too bad your ex-girlfriend spoiled things. It was fun while it lasted. You are a very special man. I will not tell Leo this, but you tempt me to leave him. I would not mind being married to you, at least for a while. However, your Nancy would not like it. Thank you for being so sweet."

Jake's hand dropped to his side. "That's it," he said, looking ready to cry.

Nancy took a step toward him. "Jake, I'm so sorry it turned out this way. I really am. I didn't want you to get hurt." She gave him a hug. He hugged her back, burying his face in her shoulder.

When they parted, he said, "Thanks, Nan, I'm okay, I think. It's just that . . . how could I not have seen it? Was I that blind?"

"Jake," Nancy said soothingly, "you were in love."

Jake cleared his throat. When he spoke again, he sounded more like himself. "Love aside, I'm supposed to be a reporter. And I just can't figure it out. Why? Why now? Why was Nadia in such a hurry? Do you get it, Nancy?"

"I only have hunches, Jake. Gail would never approve it as a story." She smiled. "It's all guesswork and little hard fact."

"Well, I'm glad I won't be reading it on the front page of the *Wilder Times*. Tell me what you've got."

Nancy paused, wondering whether this was the time or the place to go into Nadia's secret plan. Jake had the right to know, she decided. "Nadia—or Elena—came here as part of the smuggling operation. She needed some way to stay after her visa ran out."

"But that wouldn't have been for a while," protested Jake. "Why the hurry?"

"That's where Leo comes in. Nadia had a chance to come to Wilder, but Leo must not have been able to come with her. So Nadia decided to solve her own problem first. She could marry a citizen and then bring Leo over, claiming he was her brother. I think she figured she could con her American husband into supporting him."

"Go on. It sounds like you're on the right track."

"I don't think her second marriage was supposed to happen so quickly, but Leo must have gotten his chance to come here and he had to leave right then. Leaving Russia may not be as hard as it used to be, but it still takes money. And Nadia and Leo were black marketeers. It's likely the government was wise to them and they had to leave secretly. So Nadia had to find a husband right away in order to give her 'brother' a place to stay."

"That's some story. Boy, do I feel stupid." Jake studied the toes of his cowboy boots.

"Don't be so hard on yourself, Jake," Nancy said. "It wasn't your fault. She was a pro."

"Yeah, right. Well, I've got to go. I need to be alone."

"Okay, Jake. Take it easy."

"Do what you got to do," George said.

"Yeah, see you later," Bess said.

Nancy thought back to the first time she'd seen Nadia in Casey's room. "She had me fooled, too. I thought Casey had really lucked out on a roommate this time," Nancy admitted. "Now she makes Stephanie look like an angel."

"Stephanie Baur?" George said.

"An angel?" Bess's eyes popped open wide.

The girls exchanged glances, then cracked up.

After Nancy stopped laughing, she asked Bess, as casually as possible, "What are you doing for dinner?"

"Meeting Brian," Bess answered.

"You sure?" George asked.

"Look, guys, you've made your point. I confessed. But I *do* have other friends besides you two. You have to trust me, okay?"

The three friends left Nadia's room, closing the door behind them, and went their separate ways.

Nancy sat down at her desk, ready to focus on her problems. *Headlines*. She wanted to work up a new, punchier proposal for her meeting the next day with Professor Trenton and her obnoxious co-anchor.

She shuddered at the thought of Michael Gianelli as she turned on her computer. While the machine hummed as it booted up, Nancy noticed her answering machine light was flashing. "Probably one last hate message from Nadia," she mused sourly, and punched the Replay button.

"Gianelli here."

Nancy groaned. What did he want now? "Hey, Drew," his voice went on. "I've been hard at work all weekend, and I'm going to blow you away with my latest ideas for *Headlines.* Meanwhile, hope you're out doing something *flaky,* or was it *frothy?*"

"Oh, shut up!" Nancy glared at the machine and stuck her tongue out at it.

"I will not binge. I will not binge. I will not binge," Bess muttered the words as an incantation on her way to her room that night.

Rehearsal had been a mess. Everyone, including Bess, had flubbed lines, blown entrances, and set the director to screaming.

Between the debacle at rehearsal and that awful scene at the airport with Nadia and Jake, it had been one bad day. With a capital *B.*

The letter *B* reminded Bess of three things simultaneously: her own name bulimia; and the terrible urge to binge.

Bess had lied about her dinner plans with Brian. She just wasn't ready to face the real world of food yet.

She had promised Nancy. She had promised George. She had even promised herself that she would get help. But even if she meant to keep her promises, professional help wasn't available right then—unless you counted the campus hot line, which Bess preferred not to.

Music, voices, and laughter filtered through dorm room doors as she headed down the long hall toward the sanctuary of her room. Groups of people came by with nachos, chips and dip, and, sometimes, cheese puffs.

Bess's resolve weakened. Then she remembered crying all alone in the lobby bathroom. She couldn't bear the memory. "I will never, *ever* stuff myself again. Never," she said, trying to ignore the aroma of microwave popcorn.

At her door she stopped dead in her tracks. A long white box was propped against the wall. Flowers. Just seeing the box made her smile. They were probably for Leslie from Nathan.

Bess picked up the box and brought it inside their room. The note card slipped out, and Bess bent to pick it up.

To Bess, the envelope read.

"For me!" Bess gasped. She tore open the envelope and read the card.

"From your Secret Admirer."

"I don't believe this," she said to the empty room. She opened the box and looked inside. "Roses. Yards and yards of roses!" They were long-stemmed red roses at that. No one had ever sent her so many roses before.

She picked one up and breathed in its heavenly scent.

All thoughts of food rushed right out of her head. Bess was certain that the roses were a sign. A sign that something absolutely wonderful was about to happen.

NEXT IN NANCY DREW ON CAMPUS™:

Crazy. That's the word of the month at Wilder U. Like Stephanie's idea that the way to save her marriage is to have a baby. Then there's Montana throwing herself at Ray when he's not there to catch her. And talk about crazy: As if Bess didn't already have enough troubles, now she's the target of a mad bomber! Meanwhile, Nancy's co-host on the campus cable TV show is just plain *driving* her crazy. Michael is ambitious, he's stubborn, and he's so competitive. Sound familiar? A bit like . . . Nancy Drew? Maybe there's more going on between her and Michael than either cares to admit. Crazier things have happened . . . in *In the Spotlight*, Nancy Drew on Campus #24.

Nancy Drew on Campus™